The Whiteleys
of
DARNALL

SHEAF PUBLISHING   SHEFFIELD

DEDICATION

To Lydia Ann, whose era this was,

a mine of information, mostly gold!

First published in 1995 by
Sheaf Publishing Ltd,
35 Mooroaks Road, Sheffield 10

© J.W. Murfin, 1995
ISBN 185048 016 8
Printed in Great Britain

*Any resemblance in this story to any person living or dead is quite co-incidental.
There never was a Labour councillor for Darnall called Jim Whiteley, but as Darnall
people will know, there might easily have been, as the name is still very common in that
part of Sheffield. But that Sheffield Labour Party, and particularly Patience Sheard, has
over the years done much to make Sheffield a better place to live in is beyond dispute.*

The Whiteleys
of
DARNALL

John Murfin

SHEAF PUBLISHING LTD   SHEFFIELD

Chapter One

✧ ✧

T HE AIR WAS CHILL in the streets of Sheffield on that January morning in 1904. The small, plump woman pulled the shawl tighter around her head and shoulders. The high buttoned boots beneath her long black dress and coat clacked on the flagged pavement and echoed between the twin rows of smoke-blackened brick terraced houses, that lined the streets of suburban Darnall. She clutched the battered leather bag containing her instruments, her eyes shuttling a little fearfully.

It was five o'clock in the morning. The cold light of dawn was beginning to dim the gaslamps as she knocked on the door of a house, identical to all the other houses in the terrace.

She used the front door – few others did, but this woman had status of sorts, having brought most of the local children into the world. She wouldn't go down the entry into the yard like the milkman and coalman. After a shooting of bolts and rattling of chain, the door opened and she was confronted by the unprepossessing sight of Joe Whiteley.

The sleeves of the collarless union shirt that encased his stocky, muscular figure were rolled up, and at his neck could be seen the ribbed edge of a yellowed woollen vest. The lips under the ragged moustache were fixed in a grudging smile as he said, rubbing his day-old beard, 'Come in, Mrs Jordan, it's a bit parky, innit?' He ushered her into the front parlour. As he seated her on the horse-hair sofa, he asked, 'Would yer like a cupper tea while yer waitin'?'

She replied soberly, 'How often are 'er pains now, Joe?' He smoothed his moustache, an unconscious gesture, and replied, 'Ah think abaht twenty minutes. Trouble is, we 'aven't a clock upstairs.' The woman, still a bit starchy, answered, 'Right then, ah will 'ave a cup, thanks.'

Joe shouted into the kitchen, 'Joan, put t'kettle on, t'midwife's 'ere.' Joan, a pretty fifteen-year-old, stuck her head into the doorway and said, aggrieved, 'Dad, don't make so much row, you'll waken t'kids.'

Joe went across, 'Sorry lass, ah never thowt.' He dropped his voice to a stage-whisper. 'An' use t'best china.' The midwife heaved herself off the couch and headed for the kitchen.

'While you're mashin', ah'll go an' take a look at Alice. Yer know what 'appened wi' Sally, it were o'er in 'alf an hour.' She went up the steep, narrow wooden stairs to the bedroom as Joe sat down beside the grate where the kettle was coming to the boil. He lit a Woodbine. As Joan was setting out the pots, she said, 'Do yer think me mam'll be long, Dad?'

'I 'ope not, ah've got ter be at work for six o'clock, an' ah can't afford t'time

1

off, 'cos they'll gi'e me t'push.'

''S all right, Dad, ah'll stop up an' see to me mam.'

Joe, in spite of his predilection for a 'bevvy', was by the standards of the day a good husband and a good worker. He was on twelve-hour days and nights in the stampshop at Brown Bayley's, in conditions that many men would find unendurable.

Little wonder, then, that he'd be in the *Bradley Well* at Darnall tram terminus, 'pottin' up' and playing darts or dominoes while Alice sat with her half of bitter and gossiped with the other darts widows. Odd times, he would have a 'ha'p'orth' on the tram to the bottom of Staniforth Road, and go on a pub crawl, in the dozen or so hostelries down Attercliffe Road.

He'd start in the *Dog and Partridge*, and have one in every pub from there to the *Filesmith's Arms*, missing the *Traveller's* where he was banned for fighting. (One night, Bill Foster, a collier, had been chatting Alice up, and Joe had wiped the floor with him.) He'd often come home with a parcel of fish and chips for the family. This was the only meal they ever had which was not home-cooked, and it was unknown for any working people to go out to a café.

Annie Jordan came back through the door as Joan was scalding the leaves in the brown earthenware teapot with the red rubber spout. Annie's husband, Bert, had been a collier at Nunnery pit and he'd been 'in t'coil' from being twenty-one.

One day, at the age of thirty-five, when he was getting ready for work, he had said to Annie, 'Ah don't feel so grand lass, ah think ah'll 'ave one off.' It was Monday, also known as 'Saint Monday', and, consequently, many colliers took the day off. Annie replied, 'Don't pull that one, Bert. Get thissen off to work.' Ever since that day she had regretted her hasty words, for two hours into the shift, in a thirty-inch seam, the top lowered onto him. In the words of the deputy, 'A four-ton lump o' muck came down and crushed 'im. 'E were just like raspberry jam.' In those days, miners lived daily with death and injury – it went with the job.

Ever since that day she had atoned for her rash judgement by bringing new lives into the world, and she had delivered many of the kids born in the area of Darnall tram terminus. And when anyone gave up the unequal struggle for existence, Annie Jordan laid them out, straightening the contorted limbs that had fought so hard to stay in this world, getting them ready for that last, slow horse-drawn ride. The only cars that were seen on the street belonged to the doctor or the undertaker.

As she came back into the kitchen, Joe stood and asked, ''Ow is she, Mrs Jordan?' Joe's manner was stilted with strange women. He'd been brought up to believe that a woman's place was either in the wrong or in the kitchen. He remembered the saying, bandied about between men, that advised, 'Keep 'em well fed and poorly shod and they'll never leave home' – but the words weren't really 'well fed'.

The little plump woman stood foursquare, fists on hips and looked at him quizzically, then spoke with Sheffield candour.

'She's going to be awreight this time, Joe, but tha'd better mek this t'last 'un, she's just wore out.' Joe was shamefaced as he answered, gruffly, 'It's awreight thee talkin', what can ah do?'

'That's up to thee, Joe', she snapped. 'Tie a knot in it or summat. Nah get thissen off to work an' leave us women to it.' He got up and replaced his braces on his shoulders from where they hung at his sides, then hitched up the broad leather belt which went around the sensible moleskin trousers. Putting on his waistcoat, unbuttoned, he shrugged into his coat then tied his sweat-towel round his neck like a scarf. He picked up his cap and turned to Annie, saying awkwardly, 'Ah'll see thee awreight for t'money.' He turned his cap in his hands. 'Anyroad, ah'll 'ave ter get off ter work,' and putting on his cap, he beat a hasty retreat through the scullery.

'There's no 'arm in 'im, Joan, and 'e's on'y like most o' t'men round 'ere, but why can't they understand what it's like for women? Lots of us aren't allowed to enjoy it in bed, but it's us that 'ave ter suffer for it after. Men! You can't live wi' 'em and yer can't live wi'out 'em.' She picked up her cup of tea and sat beside the fire with Joan, to wait for Alice reaching her time.

It wasn't until twenty-past-eight that the time came, and Alice, with knees akimbo, bore down, to instructions from Annie Jordan. 'Come on, Alice, you've got work to do, now take deep breaths and try again. By God, 'e's a big 'un. That's it, nearly there.'

The cord was cut and tied, and the boy, for such it was, was held up by the heels and ritually slapped. At first he made no sound, but when he did, it was a bellow of rage, not a cry, as if he was angry at being dragged out into this hostile environment. In spite of his protestations, he was washed, powdered and dressed, then given to his mother. Alice, by now, had been washed and made comfortable by her daughter, who had womanfully soldiered on in spite of her quaking stomach. It was her baptism of fire, but it was all worth it as she saw the baby anxiously searching, with pouting mouth, for his mother's full breast.

★   ★   ★

Two weeks later, a procession wound its way from Kirby Road to Darnall Church. In the lead was Alice Whiteley, walking unnaturally in a long hobble-skirt, wearing a hat that she'd bought for Bert Jordan's funeral and carrying the baby. Beside her marched Joe, resplendent in blue serge and bowler hat, pulling uncomfortably at his wing collar. Just behind came Mrs Jordan, about to become a godmother for the umpteenth time, accompanied by Joan, wearing a flowered dress and broad-brimmed hat, trimmed with impossible flora.

Bringing up a reluctant rear, and wearing the clothes they got for Whitsuntide, came the other three kids: Sam, twelve years; Sally, nine and a half; and Tom, at four, happily walking with one foot in the rain-filled gutter. A brewer's dray rattled past over the granite setts, the driver giving a salute to the cortège with his raised whip.

Waiting outside the church were Joe's two brothers, each accompanied by his respective spouse, and Ted Naylor, Alice's brother, a confirmed bachelor. There were handshakes all round and the women kissed each other self-consciously as they held on to their hats in the breeze. The parson came to the door of the church in his robes and gently beckoned them in. The procession, now sober, entered the house of God.

They assembled at the font, and Annie, as the godmother, handed the priest the baby, who was by now loudly protesting.

'James Henry Whiteley', intoned the priest, 'I baptise you in the name of the Father', *splash*, 'and of the Son', *splash*, 'and of the Holy Ghost, amen.' The last splash was the final straw, and James Henry bellowed his tiny rage at this indignity.

The rest of the party sat in the front pews after the service while Alice retired with the vicar to undergo the indignity of 'churching'. After this archaic ritual the ordeal was over and they all repaired to the house in Kirby Road.

Set out in the parlour was a sit-down tea prepared by the next-door neighbour, Mrs Burrows. The heavy green brocade tablecloth with the tassels round the edge had been removed and replaced by a white cotton sheet, doubling as a tablecloth. Around the table were the teaplates, each with a slice of boiled ham – 'funeral meat' as it was known. Weddings or funerals were the only times that most families were lucky enough to enjoy this delicacy.

The family sat down to eat and the cadaverous Mrs Burrows brought round tea in the best china – an heirloom from Alice's mother. Before they began to eat, Joe, in an unexpected burst of religious fervour, said 'Grace' and surprised everyone.

*   *   *

During the following years, this nine-pound twelve-ounce morsel of humanity, labelled James Henry – James from his grandfather, and Henry from a remote uncle in Canada – grew up strong and quick of mind, in spite of major catastrophes like measles, whooping-cough and scarlet fever. He escaped the all-too-common rickets, maybe because of frequent trips up into the high ground of High Hazels Park in company with Alice.

Rickets was the curse of working-class children in Sheffield until the late 1930s, where the noxious outpourings of the hundreds of factory chimneys created a pall over the city like a crust on a pie. The healing sunshine never reached the mean streets and the families of working people living to the north and east of Sheffield were all too often imprisoned by the apathy of poverty. To be born into these surroundings was a life sentence, often a short one – the life expectancy was around fifty.

Jimmy was an adventurous lad who explored the area comprehensively. On various occasions he was lost in Tinsley Park Woods, fell into the Waverley Brook, and once was found picking willow herb on the railway lines at the end of the street. Except for masses of scar tissue on knees and elbows, his escapades left him undamaged and a little wiser.

When he was five, his mother, feeling that it was the right thing to do, broached the subject of Sunday School to Joe. Though not a regular church-goer herself, she yet thought it would be good for James Henry's soul, and she said so to her husband.

'It'll be nice for 'im to go and see if 'e takes to it. He'll meet other kids, and they have outin's an' that.' Joe, torn from his study of the racing form, dis-missed it, childhood memories of being forced to go to chapel with a religious uncle still rankling.

'Ah don't know, Alice', he said, peering over his spectacles. 'What's tha tryin' to do wi' 'im, 'e's awreight as 'e is. Why change 'im?'

'It's a good thing for all kids to go an' find out if they like it.' Joe generally took the line of 'Owt for a quiet life'.

'Ah'll leave it to thee lass, but ah can't see 'im takin' to it – 'e's a rough little bugger, an' stubborn when 'e's that way aht', and he returned to studying form.

One fateful Sunday, his mother, overriding Jim's objections, took him to Darnall Church Sunday School. Other mothers were converging on the termi-nus with similar infants destined for indoctrination. As they walked toward the church the cattle were being driven along the cobbles of the main road on their way to the Shambles in Sheffield. The animals complained as they were whacked on the rump by the drover's sticks, and left their deposits, steaming with the smell of the country, on the granite setts which had been smoothed over the years by the passage of iron-shod wheels and hooves.

Following them would come the slatted carts containing masses of large pink pigs, each cart covered by a heavy rope net. The unfortunate creatures seemed to realise that they were on their way to become pork chops, and gave voice accordingly. Lamenting their fate, they thrust swill-encrusted snouts between the slats, crying for help. Up Irving Street they would go, to the slaughterhouse behind the *Bradley Well* pub.

Scrubbed and shining, our hero was dragged past this enticing activity, and this is where the iron entered his soul. It was one of the high spots of his week 'helping' the drovers take their charges on their final journey.

Darnall at that time was still almost a village, out on the edge of Sheffield, and retained a village atmosphere. It was bounded on three sides by country-side: Tinsley Park Woods, Bowden Houstead Woods, and a huge area of farm-land on the other side of the main railway line from the south. The tram route that went down Staniforth Road was an umbilical cord linking Darnall with Mother Sheffield and the industrial complex of Tinsley and Templeborough.

Reaching the Sunday School, the women waited, each with their best bonnet on, for the doors to open. To their children went the dire warnings: 'Do yer want a wee before yer go in'; 'Be'ave thissen in theer'; and 'Stop fidgeting an' stand still'. Some used the ultimate deterrent: 'Wait till yer father 'ears about it'.

The church doors were opened by Miss Penrose, a tall, grey-haired spinster, her coiffure severely confined in a bun. The children filed in, with last-minute stroking down of unruly hair and pulling up of knitted stockings, gartered at the knee. One prim little madam was placed next to Jim on one of the hard forms. When they were all seated, everyone sang *Jesus wants me for a Sunbeam*.

Trying hard to be sociable, Jim asked the flaxen-haired minx, 'Wheer does tha live?' He was told that her name was Mary, and she lived in one of the better houses up on Oliver's Mount. He also learned that at their house they could afford ready-sliced bread, tinned fruit and holidays at Cleethorpes. Jim, having the soul of a commoner, and intolerant of females anyhow, could no longer endure this arrant snobbery and pinched her on the bottom. Her cries of injury and indignation attracted the attention of Miss Penrose, who summarily ejected the trouble-maker from the company.

Little did Jim know that this was an important event in his life: thirteen years later, he was to pinch the same girl on the same bottom for different reasons and with entirely different results. On his way home Jim made his way to the slaughterhouse to join the other little monsters listening to the pigs being killed. In the process, he slipped down on the odorous droppings, and arrived home smelling less than fragrant.

He was lucky, insofar as his father, after a morning on his allotment, had departed for his liquid refreshment with a large pom-pom in his buttonhole. Instead of summary punishment with his father's belt, he simply received a talking-to from his mother – which, even so, could reduce him to tears when the belt couldn't.

Alice, a gentle and dignified woman, had been beautiful when she was younger, and this beauty still lingered in the soft, vulnerable mouth and the lustrous brown eyes whose long lashes owed nothing to cosmetic engineering. Her crowning glory was a mass of gently-waving auburn hair which was normally coiled in a bun, held up by a large tortoiseshell comb. Let down, it fell to her waist.

Jim walked into the kitchen, blithely forgetful of the state of his backside. His mother looked down at him from mixing the batter for the Yorkshire pudding, and said suspiciously, 'Yer 'ome early, Jimmy, what 'appened?'

Jim, in an attempt at diplomacy, replied, 'Miss Penrose said she didn't need me an' sent me 'ome.' Alice's suspicions were confirmed and she demanded,

'What 'appened, Jimmy?' in ominous tones. Jim, cornered, owned up to his assault on Mary. He added, a little shame-faced, but with the ghost of a grin, 'Ah pinched 'er bum'. His mother lamented, tears in her voice. 'Oh, Jimmy, yer've shown me up again. Ah'll never be able to face t'neighbours.' Then, sniffing, 'Ave you been up to that slaughter'ouse again?' Turning him round, she discovered his secret. 'Get in that scullery an' take 'em off, yer dirty little devil. Ah've told yer till ah'm sick o' tellin' yer, yer mustn't . . . ' and much more in the same vein, reducing Jim to abject sorrow.

His misery was soothed, however, by the prospect of Sunday dinner – roast beef and two vegetables, with Yorkshire pudding. The joint had been bought by Joe the previous evening in the Shambles by the light of acetylene torches. A canny Yorkshireman, he knew that the butchers, unable to freeze the meat, auctioned it off for a fraction of the price when it got late. The potatoes and cauliflower were from the allotment, as was the rhubarb in the pie for after.

At two-thirty on the dot Joe returned from his dinner-time session, jovial with five pints of Stones' best bitter under his belt. It was known locally as 'feightin' beer', and would have put today's feeble brews to shame.

'That ale int' *Bradley* were like wine today', he said as he removed his coat and waistcoat and picked up the carving knife. As he began carving the rolled brisket, he went on, 'Ah gi'en 'em a thrashin' at crib this dinner, took 'alf a crown off 'em', and he chuckled in retrospect. Alice looked up from mashing the potatoes and asked, 'Who were yer playin'?'

'Jack Shaw an' that weedy son o'r 'is, ah think 'e must be t'recklin' o' t'litter.' Joan, coming in from the outside toilet, heard the remark and the look that she directed at her father's broad back could have pierced straight through him. Her eyes spat fire but her mother, always the peacemaker, implored her with a look. Alice knew that Joan and the gawky Bob Shaw were walking out but it was still on the secret list, Bob being three years Joan's junior. Quietly, she remarked, 'His mother says they think t'world of 'im at Tinsley Park. They were talkin' about puttin' 'im in to learn shot-firin'.' Joan could contain herself no longer.

'He's a good grafter, Dad. You shouldn't pull 'im to pieces like that.' Her father looked at her, his face still serious, but the brown eyes held a twinkle as he answered, 'Ah well, 'e seems a decent lad, Joan, an' 'e can 'old 'is ale wi' t'best o'r 'em.' He went back to his surgery on the joint.

'Yes', said Joan, 'but 'e on'y drinks for t'company.' Joe laughed. 'Aye, that's what they all say, but ah didn't see 'im leave any in 'is pot.' He put out the meat on the plates, then chuckled indulgently. 'Ah, 'e's not a bad un lass, but tek thi time, 'e's on'y a young un.'

As Alice went to the scullery door Sam – now a tall well-built seventeen-year-old – burst in with a football under his arm.

'Sorry ah'm late, Mam, we 'ad to play extra time – but we licked 'em.' She smiled, 'I'm glad yer won, Sam', and she slapped him playfully. 'Now 'urry up, yer dinner's ready.'

She called out into the yard. 'Come on in you lot, dinner's out.' The other three children erupted into the scullery, fighting to be first to the big stone sink. Alice singled Jimmy out for attention. 'Wipe yer nose.' Then, too late, 'Not on your sleeve, yer little devil.'

Everyone settled at the table and for the next ten minutes there was silence, except when Joe remarked, 'This meat's bloody lovely, Alice, an' it on'y cost me three bob'. Jimmy piped up through a mouthful of Yorkshire pudding, 'Miss Penrose at t'Sunday School says that's swearin'.'

Defensively, Joe retorted, 'Don't talk at t'table, 'specially wi' yer mouth full, or yer'll get yer arse tanned.' Jimmy, suitably chastened, went back to his plate, and silence once more descended. After the rhubarb pie had been demolished, the kids disappeared to destinations unknown, with Tom complaining, 'Do we 'ave ter tek Jimmy wi' us, Mam? 'E's nowt but a blummin' nuisance.'

'Look, 'e's yer brother, let 'im play wi' yer.' Back in the house, Joe was taking off his tie.

'Ah'm goin' ter get me 'ead dahn, Mother. Gi' me a shout abaht five o'clock, ah've said we'll be in t'*Bradley* for seven ter get some seats.'

'Right.' She gave him a peck. 'An' don't drop yer trousers on't floor.'

Chapter Two

✵ ✵

WHITBY ROAD SCHOOL was a revelation to the young Jimmy when he went there first in 1913 but, after a rebellious first twelve months, he began to enjoy it. Some of the rebelliousness remained, but much of his energy was channelled into learning and he soaked up knowledge like a sponge. His writing – in that age of copperplate script – was atrocious, and this didn't endear him to his teachers. If they had overlooked his scribble they'd have found that he possessed a very good vocabulary which was in evidence in the stories he wrote. He was forced to keep this passion for knowledge inside himself, but he read, and remembered.

Meantime, the German Kaiser's dreams of conquest drove him to invade France. Britain, in a costly display of altruism, declared war on their old allies, the Weimar Republic. The future hopes of each nation – its youth – were placed on the line, and the two juggernauts clashed. The arena that they chose was Flanders, and thus started four years of the dirtiest warfare that mankind had ever known.

Posters went up on the hoardings, pictures of a handlebar-moustached Kitchener pointing a finger and saying YOUR COUNTRY NEEDS YOU. Young men flocked to the call, and among them was Sam, eighteen ten days after the war started. Hypnotized by the jingoistic propaganda, Sam, who had no permanent female companions, gladly signed up for the King's shilling. Later, in 1916, went Bob Shaw, conscripted amid tearful goodbyes from Joan.

Jimmy would spend minutes at a time gazing at the compelling poster, seeing the finger pointing to him, from whatever angle he viewed it. Even at eleven years old, it made him feel vaguely guilty that he was unable to obey it.

It was a great occasion when Sam came home on leave before departing to France, and he cut a brave figure in his uniform. Alice, her throat swelling with pride, paradoxically felt her heart sink as she realised that her son was going into unknown dangers. For eighteen years she had always been around, whatever happened – she had patched his wounds, cheered him in defeat, and defended him even when she knew he was wrong. From now on, this handsome young man would be ploughing a lonely furrow, and all she could do was pray that he would return safe – and whole.

With Joe and Sam, however, the relationship had changed. For one thing, Sam began to contradict his father, where before he would have accepted his opinion. His uniform seemed to fuel his ego, and he strutted like a fighting cock. One day, as they were having a pint together, Joe asked conversationally, 'What are tha thinkin' o' doin' when tha comes out o' t'army? Ah could get thee a job at Brown Bayley's in t'forge.'

Sam laughed, as he sat, glass in hand. 'Yer must be jokin', Dad. When ah come out o' the army, ah'm goin' to make somethin' o' meself. You've been daft all yer life, workin' for a gaffer. Ah'm goin' to work for number one.' He swigged his beer.

Joe gazed at his son as if he didn't recognize him and, nettled, said, 'There's nowt wrong wi' an honest shillin' for an honest hour, an' you kids 'as never wanted for owt.'

Sam put a hand on his dad's shoulder. 'Yes, but it could 'a been a lot better if yer'd got yer feet out o' t'rut, couldn't it? Believe me, Dad, yer'll get nowt wi' bein' honest.'

Joe, although boiling inside, held his tongue for Alice's sake. He drank up his pint. 'Well, ah've 'ad enough, ah'm goin' 'ome an' get me 'ead down for an hour. Thee stop 'ere if tha wants', and he stumped out, a baffled man. It was the last drink they had together before Sam had to go to join his regiment, bound for the Western front.

★   ★   ★

The months went by and things settled down. However, through newspapers, the occasional dire telegram and by word of mouth – mainly from soldiers invalided out – the seriousness of the conflict was driven home. The papers had been predicting a short war, but this began to seem increasingly optimistic.

Joan, who was working at the chip shop on the terminus, came home one night in high excitement. As she put a parcel of chips on the hob, her mother asked, 'What's got into yer, Joan? Yer full of it.'

'Jenny Dodsworth come in tonight, an' she's got another job, wi' a lot more money. She's been set on at Hadfield's, turnin' shell-cases for t'army. For a month, she gets two pound a week, then she'll go on piece-work. Some on 'em are gettin' as much as fifty bob a week.'

Alice had poured a cup of tea, and she handed it to her daughter.'That's all right, but yer've got a good job already.'

'Mam, yer don't call that a good job, do yer? I'm on'y on fifteen bob a week.' She took a sip of tea, and went on, eyes sparkling. 'I could save enough to get married when Bob comes out o' t'army. We might get us-selves a little shop.' Her excitement was infectious, and she carried Alice along on the tide of her enthusiasm.

'It'd be lovely', said Alice, 'Missus Morton bought that lock-up when 'er Jack died – yer know, from that big insurance they 'ad. It on'y cost 'er eighty-five quid, an' she 'ad enough left for an 'oliday at Southport. Ah saw 'er t'other day – in a cab, if yer please – an' that must've cost 'er ten bob at least.'

'Ah'm surprised you an' me dad 'aven't got summat afore now – 'e's on good money.' Her mother sighed and shook her head.

'Ah, but 'e likes 'is ale too much. Apart from that, 'e says when 'e walks out o' them gates, 'e's 'is own gaffer. 'E doesn't want responsibility, an' ah don't blame 'im. Wait till yer get your shop, yer'll get fed up o' people comin' ter t'back door for a loaf, or twopenn'orth o' pot 'erbs.'

'Aye, but just imagine if me dad 'ad a beer-off, 'e'd drink all t'profits.'

Alice got the chips off the hob and they sat and had supper, talking over the might-have-beens and the could-bes, then went off to bed. Joe would be home at half-past-six and he'd want his breakfast.

*   *   *

At twenty-five-past-six Joe came in. Alice, knowing her husband's reluctance to converse when he came in off nights, said a quiet, 'Mornin' Joe', and was rewarded with a grunted, 'Mornin' Mother', as he sat down and ate the bread and dripping. By twenty to seven he was in bed and she prepared for the other kids getting up. First, she washed the front step and whitened it with donkey-stone. There was a competition in the street, as all the housewives tried to be the first to get the front step done.

Tom was the first up – he'd got a job taking barrowloads of coal round for old Len Goodwin in the station yard. Next, at half-past-seven, came Jimmy, who supplemented his Saturday penny with a paper round. Lastly was Sally, who worked behind the counter at Fieldsend's pawnbroker's at Darnall terminus.

When they were all away, Alice sat down with a welcome cup of tea, and sure as fate, Lily Burrows smelled it, knocked on the door and let herself in. Resignedly, Alice got up and poured another cup. As always, Lily was full of trouble – her own and other people's – but at least she was company. When Arthur, Lily's husband, had died, Alice, out of the kindness of her heart, went out of the way to help the grieving widow. To be quite honest, there had been times when she had regretted her impulsive soul. Joe swore that Lily knew the funeral service backwards and memorised the obituary column every day in the *Sheffield Telegraph*. Certainly, if you wanted to know anything about anybody in Darnall, Lily was the one to ask. Settled in a chair with a cup of tea, she launched into her repertoire.

"Ey, did you 'ear about young Albert Carr – yer know, 'is mother lives on Coventry Road, next door to t'*New Inn*.' Alice nodded wordlessly. When Lily was in full spate it was a monologue.

'Well, t'other day, when t'milkman come, 'e couldn't get any answer, so 'e popped 'is 'ead in t'door'. She became dramatic and her voice dropped a tone. 'And there she was, laid out on the floor. She'd got a letter in 'er 'and an' when t'milky looked at it 'e saw on t'top "War Office".' Her tone became funereal. 'Albert was killed at Mons . . .' Her voice lightened. "Er 'air turned white overnight, snow-white, poor woman.' She paused. 'Then that bloke as used ter bring t'firewood round, 'e were in t'army an' 'e lost a leg, an . . .' Alice broke in.

'Lily, don't yer think yer could pick a different subject', and she looked pointedly at Sam's picture, high on the mantelpiece. Lily was unabashed.

''Ow is Sam, by the way? Ave y'eard from 'im lately?' Alice stood up and reached onto the mantelpiece with its fringed red pelmet, and handed over a card. The front of it was covered with flower-embroidered lace and in a pocket was a tiny lace handkerchief. Lily turned it over and read the back, her lips moving. She looked up.

'It doesn't say where 'e is.' She handed the card back.

'No, it doesn't, 'e's just somewhere in France.' Alice re-read the card, her eyes misty, then replaced it.

Lily sipped her tea, then said, 'What do yer think abaht t'rent goin' up, then? Three-an'-ninepence is a lot for these 'ouses, but the owd sod 'as to 'ave 'is pound o' flesh – another thre'pence if yer please. Ah think it's outdacious.' She continued her tirade against the establishment in this way, sparing no-one.

After two cups of tea she finally got up to go – to a sigh of relief from Alice – and explained, 'Ah must get off. Ah'm takin' some flowers dahn to t'cemetry. It's four years since Arthur died.' She paused, her finger on the sneck. 'Still, it gets me aht for an hour.'

On her own once more, Alice scrubbed the front and back steps and did them with a donkey-stone, then went and cleaned the outside toilet. The board seat with the hole in it was scrubbed white but she scoured it once more and hung up fresh pieces of newspaper on the string.

As she came out of the 'closet', as it was known, carefully stepping over the newly-whitened step-stone, Jimmy came in from school. She questioned him with the probing gaze of a mother. ''Ave you been in trouble again?'

He shuffled his feet. 'Ah got t'cane again, Mam.'

'Bad writin'?' Her look was searching.

'Aye.' The boy paused, then brightened. 'But t'teacher said it were t'best composition in t'class, then 'e g'en me t'stick.' Alice emptied the bucket down the grate in the middle of the yard and said, 'It serves yer right, yer'll 'ave ter try 'arder', and she took the bucket into the scullery.

Jimmy demolished two doorsteps of bread and dripping and a mug of cocoa, and left once more for school in a cloud of dust. Alice watched him go with a wry smile. Really, she was proud of this final fruit of her womb, this cheerful, effervescent ball of fire that no-one would tame. Given good reason they might lead him, but he would never be driven.

Joe was up at two o'clock and as he sat with his pint pot of tea, putting on his boots he told his wife, 'Ah'm just poppin' across t'road ter put a bet on, ah wain't be long'. He put his coat on, and in his flat cap and a muffler, set off to Mick Thompson's on Irving Street. He got a nod from the lookout standing outside Barber Baines' on the corner then, halfway up the street, he turned down the entry into the yard.

Mick was in the kitchen, all very business-like. He took the bet and put the slip in an aspidistra pot on the table. If the lookout signalled that a 'rozzer' was coming, that pot would be under the seat in the closet, beside the 'soil' bucket, and the bookie would be over the wall into Davy's yard. Joe's bet was a 6-4-1 and came to two-and-threepence. He handed over the money and left while Mick grinned, thinking that there was one born every minute, and put the bet down in his book.

Periodically, in spite of his security precautions, the wily Mick *was* caught out, and he would be seen being ushered into the Black Maria. The policeman, looking throttled in his high-necked uniform and helmet, would follow with heavy tread, and with the aspidistra pot under his arm for evidence. The door of the ominous conveyance would close on Mick, and his touts too, if they could catch them. The driver, high on the seat at the front of the van, would crack his whip and they would be away to Attercliffe Police Station and durance vile. Up before the 'beak', they'd be sent 'dahn t'spike' for a few days and honour would be satisfied. There were rules to the game that were observed by both sides, and a 'fair cop' was accepted.

Joe, coming out of the entry, made his way to the *Bradley Well* for a 'quick un', and Nobby, behind the bar, started pulling him a pint of bitter as soon as he walked in. Any bloke who drank mild was a bit strange in that district of hard drinkers, and to be seen with a shandy was the ultimate degradation – shandy was for women. In Darnall, if you drank with the men, you supped your ale and paid your corner, but anyone who was temporarily skint could depend on his mates buying him one. To these people at this time the ale took the place of today's Librium tablets as a relief from worry. If you got too bad, the green van came from Middlewood Asylum and took you away.

Nobby picked up his fag from the edge of the bar, where the mahogany was decorated with a row of burns, and remarked, 'Don't often see yer in 'ere at dinner when yer on neets, Joe. What's up, couldn't tha sleep?'

'Ah've just been puttin' a bet on at Mick's, an' ah thowt ah could just do wi' a pot.' He took out a Woodbine and held it up for a light from the landlord's cigarette. Nobby, leaning on the bar, lit it, saying, 'We sell matches, tha knows.'

Joe, with a straight face, retorted, 'Think thissen lucky ah paid thee for t'ale. Ah don't think tha's cleaned t'pipes aht sin' Easter', and he drifted over to watch the dart players. Nobby shook his head, po-faced and quite unperturbed, and returned to studying form, squinting through the smoke from his cigarette.

As her husband came into the kitchen, Alice said, 'It took thee long enough to put a bet on'. Joe put his coat over the chair back and explained,

'Just fancied a pot in t'*Bradley*, so nah ah'll get me 'ead dahn for an hour.' He unlaced his boots. 'When Jimmy comes in, tell 'im to bring a late *Star*, ah'd like to see t'results.' Alice busied herself getting the tea ready. It was Friday, and Joe didn't get paid until he went to work, so it was stew and dumplings.

Jimmy came in as she was peeling the potatoes, so she passed on Joe's orders. Clutching the money for the paper importantly because of this special assignment, he said, 'Tara, Mam, ah'll see you in a bit', and he dashed off to earn his coppers.

★   ★   ★

At five o'clock Alice woke her sleeping spouse. As he was sitting down to a heaped plate, Jimmy came in, breathless.

'Here, Dad, ah've brought yer t'paper. Mester Williams let me 'ave it for nowt, because' ah'd gorrim two new customers.' Joe suspended operations on the vittles and turned to the stop press, searching the blotchy print for the results of his bet.

Suddenly he jumped up, his eyes lighting, 'Ah've done it, Mother', he exclaimed. 'Wait a minute', and he took a stub of pencil out of his waistcoat pocket. After some abstruse calculations on the blank patch in the stop press he sat back in his chair, unbelieving, and exclaimed,

'Do yer know, Mother, ah reckon ah've won a fortune. By my reckonin' it comes to over a 'undred quid. Mind yer, Mick's got a limit, but ah think ah'll get abaht thirty quid. Ah don't believe it.' He went back to his figures. 'See, ah'd got a ten-to-one, goin' on a seven-to-one, an' then Bad Penny past t'post at twenty-five-to-one.' He checked again. 'An' t'last un come in at thirteen-to-two it's reight tha knows!'

Alice, her eyes glowing, said, 'That's the most money we've ever 'ad in one piece, Joe. It's wonderful. What yer goin' to do wi' it?'

Her husband took his time answering this weighty question, and occupied himself absorbing more nourishment. Eventually he paused, as he considered the problem, like the head of Firth-Brown's deciding whether to put in a bid for Hadfield's.

'First of all, Alice, ah'm gonna buy thee a new coat wi' fur on t'collar.'

His wife interrupted, anxiously, 'Oh no, Joe, ah've two coats already, an' they're both alreight.'

Joe thumped the table. 'Bloody likely! We'll go up t'town an' see what they've got. Tha deserves it, lass, t'way tha puts up wi' me.'

Alice, overwhelmed, murmured, 'Thanks, Joe, but yer shouldn't.'

He went on expansively, wealth going to his head. 'An' ah'll tell thee summat else', and he turned to look at Jimmy, sitting there with his mouth open at these grand carryings-on. 'Bein' as Jimmy's t'on'y one left that's not workin', ah'm gonna buy 'im owt 'e wants.' Then he qualified his words, 'Within reason. What's tha want, Jimmy?'

The lad, in uncharted waters, stopped with a piece of dumpling halfway to his mouth, astounded at this unprecedented opportunity. After a few moment's frantic thought, he burst out, 'Ah want a pig.'

His father gazed at him dumbfounded, then almost shouted, 'Tha what?' Then more quietly, curious, 'What the 'ell does tha want a pig for?'

Jimmy went on. 'Ah on'y want a little un.' Then, seeing the expression on Joe's face, stubbornly, 'Ah want a pig. Ah want to keep it an' feed it and watch it grow till it's as big as them as comes up Irving Street in t'carts. Them blokes as brings 'em'll tell me what to do.'

It was the biggest speech he'd ever made, and he gazed hopefully at his bene-factor.

His father, still in shock, argued, 'Where tha goin' to keep it? Tha can't keep it in t'yard, can tha?' The boy persisted – this was the chance of a lifetime.

'Ah bet Mester Johnson'd let me keep it in that 'ut on t'other side o' t'railway line. 'E never uses it. Go on, Dad, ah'll look after it.' His eyes implored.

'That owd sod Johnson wouldn't gi'e thee t'snot off 'is nose-end . . . Awreight then, if thi mind's made up, ah'll get thee a pig.'

Jimmy, overwhelmed, babbled, 'Thanks, Dad, ah'll clean yer boots wi'out bein' telled, an' ah'll 'elp on t'allotment.'

'Ah'll keep thee to that', said Joe, grinning, 'an' ah'll try an' catch Ralph Meadows tomorrow dinner an' see abaht thi pig.' Jim tucked into his tea then dashed off to tell his mates about his good fortune, closely followed by his father on his way back to work with his snap tin. This had once contained tof-fees, but now held eight slices of bread and cheese and his mashings. These were twists of newspaper, each with a mix of tea, sugar and condensed milk to be brewed in his mashing can.

As he left Alice, he kissed her and confided, 'Not a word to t'others, but ah might tek t'family to t'seaside for t'day.'

At six o'clock, Joan came home, bone-weary but jubilant, still clad in her ankle-length khaki overall and cap. She showed her mother her wage-packet.

''Ow's that, Mam? Two pound seventeen-an'-ninepence.'

Alice looked and said, 'That's lovely, Joan, but don't yer think yer overdoin' it?'

'No, Mother. After tea ah'm 'avin' a bath an' ah'll be as good as new.'

'All right, if you'll get yer own tea out o' t'saucepan, ah'll be lightin' t'boiler.'

Joan lit the fire under the boiler, then went to fetch the tin bath which hung on a nail outside, beside the back door. She was putting the bath onto the rug in front of the fire when Sally returned from her day at Fieldsend's pawn-brokers and asked her sister, 'Can ah go in first, Joan? Ah'm not as mucky as you.'

An argument ensued which finished when Alice said, 'If yer don't 'urry up, Tom'll be 'ere an' then 'e'll want ter get in.'

She went to stoke up the boiler, and Sally whispered to her sister, 'Lerrus go in first, Joan, ah'm goin' out wi' Bert Thompson tonight, 'e's takin' me to t'*Palace*.'

Joan replied, equally quietly, 'Watch yourself, Sal, that Bert's already got one lass in trouble. But they couldn't prove it.'

They discontinued the conversation when Alice returned, and Sally stripped off. As Alice saw her daughter there and looked at the proud young body, she saw herself as she was twenty-five years before, when she met Joe. The first time she met the stocky, dependable-looking young man was when he came to their house in Whitby Road to buy a greyhound pup from her brother Ted, and it was love at first sight. They had walked out for eighteen months and the nearest young Joe ever got to sex was fondling one warm young breast as they sat in High Hazels Park in friendly darkness. The chastity of this relationship had not been Joe's idea, but Alice's parents were staunch churchgoers and she was brought up strictly.

However, on one fine Spring evening they lay close on the sun-warmed turf in the park and Joe's passions could no longer be contained. Alice's blood was running hot, and she was about to succumb to his pleading when boots crunched on the gravel path and the warm yellow beam of an oil lantern revealed them in their compromising position.

The light was clipped to the belt of Constable Berry, the local bobby, who had warned them, not unkindly, 'Now come on, you two, it's time you were 'ome'. Ignominiously they had walked away down the path, not even hand-in-hand. Two months later they were married at Darnall Church.

Sally completed her toilet, and Joan followed her in the bath, her heavier, full-breasted figure contrasting with her sister's lighter build. She was still extremely attractive but she was saving it all for Bob, out in Flanders.

A knock came on the door, which was bolted, and Joan, sitting in the bath, grabbed a towel while Alice went to the door.

'Is that our Tom?' The door rattled and a voice said, 'Course it is. Ah want mi tea.'

Alice retorted, 'Joan's in t'bath, so yer'll 'ave ter wait. Go an' fetch me 'arf a pound o' chitterlin's an' a link o' poloney from Armitage's.' The door opened a crack and some coins changed hands. There was grumbling from outside, then receding footsteps as a reluctant Tom carried out his orders. Joan stepped out of the bath like Aphrodite rising from the waves, and dried herself. By the time he returned she had joined Sally at the table, fully dressed. Tom was black from his labours with the coal-barrow, but his lips, where he had licked them, were pink.

His mother chuckled, 'You look like a nigger minstrel. Just wash yer 'ands and get yer tea afore t'dumplin's is like bullets.' The three got on with their meal, while Alice sat with a cup of tea and told them about Joe's good fortune. 'And 'e's buyin' me a coat, and Jimmy a pig.'

16

Sally giggled and asked, 'A pig? What does our Jimmy want a pig for?'

'He wants ter keep it an' feed it hisself.' Alice was defensive. 'It can eat what you lot leave, and it'll be worth some money when it grows up.'

The light-hearted discussion continued until Jimmy's return, at which Tom started grunting and squealing. There followed a scuffle which came to an end when their mother threatened to pour water on them. During the melée, much of Tom's coaldust was transferred to his brother, so they were given a lading can and bucket and told to empty the bath. The zinc coffin was refilled, and after another struggle for precedence, two very scruffy children were transformed.

They were imprisoned in the parlour with a pack of cards until bedtime, while Alice sat down to read. Her passion was for romantic fiction which transported her into a world far from her own. Leisured meals on the banks of the Seine and midnight rendezvous at Le Touquet with a handsome stranger were her escape. But the only river she knew was the lifeless polluted Don, and her only midnight meetings were in an old brass bedstead with a flock mattress. Her handsome stranger was a work-weary bloke who smelled of beer and fags but who, nonetheless, was inordinately proud to have the love of this gentle woman.

*   *   *

The following day, after four hours' sleep, Joe was up and about, and at half-past-eleven went down to collect his winnings. The family waited on tenterhooks. It was an hour later when Joe returned, and the atmosphere was electric as they heard him at the back door. He came into the kitchen, grinning widely and carrying a sack that wriggled and squealed.

''Ere y'are, Jim', he said, 'Yer've got yer pig.' Jimmy, speechless, squatted on the pegged rug to look into the sack at the pink, wriggling creature, and Joe went on. 'An' ther's another one in t'yard. It's no good 'avin' a lad wi'out a lass.' It was too much for Jimmy and he grabbed his father's leathery hand in both his little ones, not knowing how to show his love and gratitude to another male, least of all a fully-grown one.

'That's awreight, son', Joe said gruffly, ruffling the unruly brown hair, and turned to Alice and the rest, who waited with bated breath. Theatrically he put his hand in his pocket and threw on the table no less than seven large crisp five-pound notes. Tentatively, they reached out and fingered the big, white rectangles covered in copperplate script. They had seen them, but never owned one, yet there on the scrubbed deal table were the dreams of Croesus.

Joe placed both his thumbs in his waistcoat armholes and stated, 'An' ah'll tell yer summat else. We're all goin' on a day trip ter Skegness, after we've bought yer mother a new coat.'

There was pandemonium as they all tried to talk at once, and the pig ran

17

squealing round the kitchen, with Jimmy and Tom in hot pursuit.

Joe Whiteley turned to Alice and took her hands in his, 'You an' me luv, we're goin' up t'town fer your coat, then ah'm takin' yer to t'*Commercial* fer a port 'n' lemon, and then we're goin' to t'*Alexandra Theatre* to see Fred Karno an' Vesta Tilley.'

Squeezing his hands, she answered, 'Thanks, Joe, you're wonderful.' To cover his embarrassment he bent and grabbed the pig, stuffing it back in the sack, and told his son, 'You'll 'ave ter see Mester Johnson abaht usin' 'is shed.' Jimmy grinned cheekily as he was going out of the door and replied, 'Ah've seen 'im already, Dad, an' ah've got t'key to t'shed. Ah've got ter gi' 'im fourpence a week.'

Joe exploded. 'The mingy owd sod', then looked guiltily at his wife. 'Sorry Alice, it slipped out.'

With mock severity she snapped, 'Joe Whiteley, ah'm goin' ter wash your mouth out wi' soap an' water. Such language.'

The two lads slipped out of the door laughing, carrying their wriggling bundle. Alice went into the scullery and came back with a lading can full of hot water. As she poured it into the bath on the hearth, her husband picked up his cap. 'Well, if th'art gerrin' in t'bath, ah'm goin' fer a jar. Ah on'y 'ad one this dinner wi' messin' abaht wi' Jimmy's pigs. Tha knows, 'e might make summat at that. 'E could sell t'pigs at t'slaughter'ouse – it could be t'makin' of 'im.'

Joe put on his cap, saying, 'Ah'll see thi in abaht an hour', and he walked out of the door. Alice stood and watched him go, the lading can in both hands, and her expression betrayed just how much the man meant to her.

★   ★   ★

Dressed in her best black dress in honour of the occasion, Alice picked up the curling tongs from the hob and tested them on a piece of newspaper. Satisfied with the results of her research, she was just applying them to her hair when a knock came on the door. She replaced the tongs on the hob and opened the door, still bolted from bath-time.

'Hello, Connie', she exclaimed to the little woman who stood there. 'Come in love, you don't look up to t'mark.'

Connie Shaw, the mother of Joan's bloke, walked through the kitchen, her eyes red and puffy with weeping. Alice bent over her as she sat, and asked, compassion in her voice,

'What's up, love? 'Ad a fall out wi' t'owd man?'

'Oh, Alice', she sobbed, the tears starting to flow, 'it's Bob'. She turned up her tear-stained face. 'Ah've 'ad a letter from t'War Office. It says 'e's lost a leg through enemy action, an' they're sendin' 'im 'ome.'

She bent to her handkerchief, and Alice absently patted her back as she realised the effect that this would have on Joan. She gave the distraught woman

18

a glass of precious sherry and did her best to console her.

'At least 'e *is* comin' 'ome, Connie, that's more than can be said of a lot o' lads.'

Eventually, after Alice had listened and Connie had unburdened herself, Connie went home, if not cheerful, at least a little calmer. Half-an-hour later Joan came in from shopping and took out a parcel. 'I've bought meself a blouse, mother, on'y one-and-nine.'

Her mother put a hand on her shoulder. 'Sit down lass, ah've summat to tell thee.' Her daughter, puzzled, sank into the chair. Alice continued. 'Bob's 'ad an accident, an' they're sendin' 'im 'ome.'

Joan's expression didn't change as she said, 'Tell us t'rest mother, it's no surprise. Ah knew there were summat wrong.'

'All ah know is, 'e's lost a leg, and 'e's on his way 'ome. Ah'm sorry, love.'

Joan's expression hardened, the set of her jaw firming. 'That's it then. We'll 'ave to get that shop now.' As the girl rose, not knowing where she was going, Joe came in the door and at once sensed the atmosphere.

Alice whispered the news and he went over and put his arm around the shoulders of his first-born and murmured simply, 'Sorry, love'.

Joan could contain her emotion no longer and ran up the stairs, her tears private. Alice followed to comfort her child. Joe, nonplussed, did the automatic thing – he put the kettle on. In any disaster the universal panacea was a cup of tea, hot strong and sweet, and as he heard them returning he poured out three cups. Brewing tea was not normally a man's job.

He passed the life-giving brew to his wife and daughter, and said to Alice, his voice hesitant, apologetic, 'Do yer mind, lass, if we mek it another day. It wouldn't be reight, goin' aht when . . .'

Joan, now reconciled, broke in. 'No Dad, ah'll be all right, you get off an' enjoy yersen. No, go on', she continued, as her father started to interrupt, 'it's not often yer can go mad'. Reluctantly, the pair decided to carry on with their plans, and away they went to catch a tram at Darnall terminus.

The terminus was where the tram-drivers, using a long hooked pole, swapped the trolley from one end of the tram to the other, while the conductor reversed all the slatted wooden seats. Blue sparks crackled in the air above the tramcar as the trolley re-engaged the wire, just as it did for no obvious reason when there was frost on the wires.

There is a street in Paris, the Rue de la Paix, and it's said that if you sit at its sidewalk cafés long enough, you will meet anyone in the world. As with the street in Paris, if you stayed long enough at Darnall terminus, everyone in Sheffield would pass you, including some you'd rather not see.

Situated at the junction of four roads, the terminus was the heart, the soul of Darnall. On the junction, in the middle of the road, was a monument to Victorian engineering, which – on account of there being six pubs within easy staggering distance – was one of the most frequently patronised places in Darnall. Known as the 'Iron Duke', it was an ornate, cast-iron, gent's urinal, and it was the pivotal point of this grimy carousel, the landmark, the rendezvous, friend, shelter, and comfort to the traveller.

Within a hundred yards of this temple of hygiene one could catch a train, board a tram, hear a sermon or find female companionship, and, in the many little shops, buy anything from a loaf to a mangle. Around the octagonal structure and its accompanying gaslamp, children played safely and old men squatted with their pipes, leaning against its friendly bulk as they watched the passing show. It was Darnall's male bastion from birth to death.

★   ★   ★

Late that night, after a wonderful day in the big city, Joe and Alice sat close on the uncomfortable wooden seats, as the electric juggernaut rocked and rattled its way along the shining rails. Alice, like a young girl, hugged the arm of her husband, his bowler at a rakish angle, as they chatted happily about the show. They disembarked at Ronald Road and strolled back to the little house in Kirby Road; for them there was no tomorrow, only a wonderful today.

That night, in the old brass bedstead on that lumpy old flock mattress, she thanked her man the best way she knew, and she was eighteen again.

Chapter Three

❋ ❋

S UNDAY DAWNED bright and clear and Joe was up and about, Jimmy not
far behind him. Alice was up before either and they sat down to a steaming plate of hash to sustain them in their labours.

The lad had been round at the neighbours' houses the previous evening,
cadging leftovers for his pigs, and he was on his way to feed them. His father,
as he wiped his plate with one of Alice's breadcakes, said, 'On me way to
t'allotment, ah might as well call an' 'ave a look at yer pigs.'

Jimmy's chest swelled. '*Your* pigs' his father had said – they were *his* pigs; he
was a man of property.

The two Whiteleys walked up Acres Hill Road and over the old iron bridge,
their footsteps echoing hollowly. As they crossed, the eight-thirty from Victoria Station panted its way beneath them, slowing for the station at Darnall. The
train smell, acrid and sulphurous, came up between the boards and stung their
nostrils. It was evocative, even to Joe, of faraway places, their only connection
with a big, unknown world.

Reaching the rickety shed, patched with enamel adverts for Rowntree's
Cocoa and Gossage's Soap, the lad importantly unlocked the big padlock, carefully opened the door a crack, then dodged in, followed by his father. The pigs,
not used to their new master, ran around squealing, but soon settled down,
snuffling at the mess in the old enamel bowl. Jim, already the farmer, stood
with fists on hips. 'They'll be awreight once they settle in, Dad.'

'Ah, but yer want a run fer 'em. Ah'll tell yer what, ah've got some wire net-
tin' on t'allotment. We'll see if we can scrounge any wood fer some posts, an'
ah'll gi' yer a 'and ter build it, ther's nowt spoilin'.'

Jim, overjoyed at this attention, set off for the allotments, the town-dweller's
only connection with growing things. They reached Joe's 'little acre', a rectangle of open land that cost him a pound a year, and started hunting for materials
for their building project. The plot, when Joe took it on, had been part of someone's field and he had lifted all the grass with a spade, using it to build the cus-
tomary turf hut, roofed with corrugated sheets.

The live-wire Jimmy eagerly dashed off in search of posts while Joe made a
fire and put the old mashing can to boil, filled from the standpipe in the lane.
The chipped, navy-blue can was boiling as Jim staggered back with his arms
full. There were two bed irons, one rustic pole and three assorted pieces of
timber.

'Tha's done well, mate', exclaimed Joe, the 'mate' earning him another star
in Jimmy's book. 'Come an' get a cuppa.'

They sat down companionably in front of the fire, sharing the stewed tea, then set off back to the piggery. The posts were bundled on Joe's shoulder while Jimmy carried the spade and chicken-wire.

Arriving at their goal, the lad asked, 'Right, Dad, what do we do now?'

'First of all, pop 'ome an' look in t'cupboard under t'sink. Tha'll find me 'ammer an' a jar o' nails – an' tha'd better bring t'pincers as well.'

By eleven-thirty the compound was finished, and it even sported a gate hung on leather hinges and fastened with a loop of string. The hut door was ceremonially opened and the proud owner lovingly watched his livestock, while his father lit his eternal Woodbine.

They discussed the future of the pigs, then Joe nipped the end off his fag and put the stub in his waistcoat pocket, taking out his big, silver pocket-watch. This imposing piece of jewellry had been given to him by his father on his twenty-first birthday, a common custom in those days.

Opening the front of the watch, he said, 'Ah'm off, Jim, ah'll see yer at dinner-time, an' don't be late or yer mother'll kill yer', and he strode off in search of a 'bevvy'.

★   ★   ★

The following Tuesday evening, Joe, who was on days, was in his chair having ten minutes' nap. Joan was clearing the table and Alice was doing the pots, when there was a knock on the door.

'See who it is Joan, me 'ands is wet.' Alice watched as her daughter opened the door, her mouth forming a greeting. The girl froze, and her mother saw her colour drain as she looked at the unseen caller. She swayed, and with visible effort stepped forward with arms outstretched. Alice wiped her hands on her apron as Joan reappeared, leading the gaunt figure of Bob Shaw.

Always gawky, Bob was now painfully thin, his face the colour of uncooked pastry as he stood, slightly bent, resting on wooden crutches. His right trouser-leg was pinned-up, six inches above where his knee should have been. He turned to Alice.

'I'm sorry, Missis Whiteley.' His voice had lost much of its Sheffield twang. 'I came home this mornin' but I knew Joan wouldn't be in so I left it till now.' It had taken him until now to pluck up courage to face the girl that he had promised to marry.

'That's all right, Bob, we're glad to see you anytime.' Alice's expression held a mother's compassion. Then, business-like, she continued to Joan, 'Take Bob into t'front room an' ah'll bring yer a cup o' tea.'

The couple went into the parlour and the door closed behind them. Alice shook Joe's shoulder and when he opened bleary eyes she whispered news of their visitor. He laced his boots and did up his waistcoat.

Later, she took in the tea and some home-made cake. As she entered the parlour, the two were sitting self-consciously holding hands and wearing a strained expression.

'My, ah didn't know it was as dark as this', Alice exclaimed. She was back in a moment with a burning spill and held it up to the gas mantle. She pulled the chain and the room was flooded with the bright glare.

'Now, drink your tea before it's cold', she said, and bustled out, leaving them to their privacy.

She and her husband settled down in the kitchen to wait, and when the lovers emerged Joan seemed more confident and Bob much improved. They stood hand-in-hand as Joe put down his paper and took off the wire-framed spectacles he had bought from Woolworths. The girl smiled and said, looking at both her parents, 'We've made our minds up, we're still getting married'.

Seated in a straight-backed chair, Bob explained, 'We're puttin' together my gratuity an' Joan's savings and lookin' round for a shop. My dad works on t'market an' 'e might get us some stuff wholesale.'

Joan took over. 'You see, we're thinkin' of a tobacconist's and papers, an' we can sell bits an' bats o' fancy stuff. Bob'll get a false leg in a couple o' weeks, an' 'e'll be able to get around better.' She ran to Alice and they both wept glad tears as Bob and Joe shook hands.

Joe promised, 'Get a shop on New'all Road, an' ah'll guarantee that most o' Brown Bayley's'll get ther fags theer, but ah'll expect some commission.' He walked over to the sideboard and came up with a bottle of Haig's whisky and four glasses.

As he poured the drinks he said, 'We've 'ad this in t'cupboard for three year, so it ought ter be good', and they drank a toast to the new business.

As for the wedding, it would be a couple of months before it came about. As Bob said, 'I mustn't fall down in t'aisle, I'll 'ave to get used to t'pot leg.'

Later, in the *Bradley*, Bob was the hero and was called on to explain how he came to be 'one short'. 'We went over the top. I'd had a swig o' the rum bottle, an' on the way across I copped a piece o' shrapnel in me leg.' He tapped his stump. 'I went down in a crater an' laid there for forty hours. By the time they found me, me leg'd gone gangrene so they put me out. When I come round, there it were – gone.'

Needless to say, Bob didn't pay for a drink that night and was escorted home by his new family.

*   *   *

Friday arrived, and everyone was agog as Saturday drew near, the day of the big trip. All the family had bathed and all the clothes, newly-pressed, were laid out for morning. Alice and the girls brushed their hair until it shone, while the boys cleaned the boots and were packed off to bed early. Joe went to the beer-off and came back with five bottles of beer and four of lemonade, the latter with glass marbles in the necks.

Not much sleep was had that night, for they were up at six to catch the seven-fifteen train for Skegness at Darnall station. Alice bustled about, hair in curlers, packing up two loaves' worth of cheese and dripping which were wrapped in greaseproof paper. In a tin was one of her cakes. All these goodies were placed in a straw shopping bag.

The entire safari was on the platform by five-past-seven, anxious to be on their way. Tom, feeling magnanimous with three-and-sixpence in the pocket of his long trousers, got two penny bars of Nestlé's chocolate out of a machine, for himself and Jimmy. At long last, the excursion train gasped its way into the station. Its coaches had seen better days, but to them it was the Orient Express to Venice, and they piled aboard. Each mile of the journey in the crowded coach was an adventure, but after an hour everyone was thirsty, and the bottles were passed out with one sandwich each.

The boys shared one bottle of pop and Jimmy took first drink through a mouthful of bread and dripping, then passed the bottle to his brother, with bits of sandwich floating in it. Tom guzzled, uncaring, while Alice and the girls sipped primly at the bottles of beer as if it was Darjeeling tea in bone china. Joe drank heartily, laying a foundation for future libations in Skegness.

After many 'oohs' and 'aahs' from Sally and the boys, Tom, stationed at the window, asked, ''Ow long shall we be now, Dad?' Joe consulted his trusty timepiece. 'We ought to be theer in ten minutes.'

When the train finally pulled into Skegness station, the party disembarked with their bags and trooped down Lumley Road, gazing at everything with eyes of wonder. Walking on the front they saw the peep-shows, the bearded lady, the dog with two heads and the human skeleton, and they tried unsuccessfully to dislodge those infuriating coconuts. Joe bought a jug of tea and they went down on the beach for a picnic. Then, while Joe went in search of the juice of the hop, the rest went paddling, Tom with his trousers rolled up and Alice and the girls holding their long skirts up to their knees.

The day went all too quickly as they sampled the exotic delights of this East Coast wonderland. Too soon they had to return to the real world, although they were taking back many happy memories. They would talk about them over and over in the long winter evenings, when the wind howled under the kitchen door and they huddled closer to the fire.

The journey home was uneventful, and very soon the others fell asleep, leaving Alice to sit watching the lights of unknown villages come out of nowhere and disappear into limbo. It was hypnotic and she allowed her imagination free rein. She saw, in her mind's eye, other mothers with similar lives to her own and was so engrossed that she drifted into slumber, only to awake with a start when a porter on the platform shouted, 'Darnall'. She hustled her sleepy brood off the train.

* *

Chapter Four

THE WEEKS of late summer 1916 went slowly by, the monotony relieved only by reports of the far-distant war being fought in places that, to the denizens of Darnall, were just names. Ypres, The Somme, The Marne were all equated in the minds of the people of this industrial hamlet with Southampton, The Severn and The Thames. All were unreachable. Then came the nights when the sirens sounded and the conflict was no longer remote. People reacted in different ways to the interuptions. Some, rebellious, stayed in their beds, whilst others preferred the open air, the cellar or under the table in the kitchen.

As time went on and the threats didn't materialise, more and more families opted for staying between the sheets, thinking, 'If anyone goes, we all go together'. Then, early one September morning, when the trees in High Hazels Park were burnished gold by autumn shades, the blow fell.

Alice, always a light sleeper, was awake at the first rising wail of the air-raid warning, and within two minutes all the family – excluding Joe, who was on night-shift – were down the cellar. Alice followed them, clutching an old hand-bag containing the family documents and they settled down to wait for the all-clear.

The daring ones who stayed put ignored the insistent howl of the sirens. Then, just as they were drifting off again into sleep, there came from above their houses an ominous, grinding roar of engines. In the experience of most people at that time, the only things that flew were birds and kites, yet here was some devilish engine of destruction right over their heads. Most elected to get nearer to Mother Earth.

In Britannia Road, down past the billiard hall, a border collie left out overnight was relieving his bladder against a gaslamp. Overhead, the bombardier in the Zeppelin, only having one bomb left, reached out and released his lethal egg. The poor collie, leg still cocked, was sent to join his ancestors, whilst the suction from twenty pounds of high explosive destroyed the front of one of the houses. The inhabitants, fortunately, were in the cellar, but the luckless collie was buried under an avalanche of bricks.

At the welcome sound of the all-clear, half of Darnall flocked to witness the effects of the airborne destruction. It brought the war to their own doorsteps, a little taste of what their sons were experiencing in the mud of Flanders.

The following day, flaring headlines in the *Sheffield Telegraph* announced, ANGEL OF DEATH HOVERS OVER DOOMED CITY. There were over a score of dead and injured, and in its path over the city the airship damaged dozens of buildings. Sheffield was now in the firing line.

★   ★   ★

The pigs grew at an alarming rate and the indefatigable Jimmy ranged far and wide foraging for their food. His gross income was threepence for his paper round and his Saturday penny, yet his outlay was fourpence for the rent. His finances were stretched to the limit. One day, when his father was in a good mood, Jim buttonholed him. Joe was reading, hiding behind his newspaper.

'Dad, do you know 'ow old I am?' Receiving no reaction, he went on, 'Ah'm thirteen in two months an' ah on'y get a penny a week'.

The paper trembled but no sound came. He gave it one more try. 'Ah cleaned yer boots an' went errands an' fetched yer paper.' For a moment nothing happened, then there was a roar of laughter and the paper came down. 'Awreight, yer little sod, ah'll mek it threepence, an' that's me last offer.'

'Thanks Dad.' Then, after a pause, and cheekily, 'Does it start las' Sat'day? Cos' it's on'y Monday.' His dad fished in his pocket, saying, 'Right, ah owe thee tuppence, tha's already 'ad a penny.'

He searched among his change and complained, 'Smallest ah've got is a thre'penny bit. Got any change, Jim?'

'I 'aven't, sorry.'

'That's it then', and he started to put it back in his pocket. But as he saw his son's face fall, he said, 'Awreight, 'ere y'are', and he passed over the tiny silver coin. The lad dashed off to pay his rent.

At half-past-eight Jimmy rolled in, looking smug and smelling of the country. His father held his nose. 'Bloody 'ell, lad, tha smells ripe.'

Jimmy grinned. 'Ah, but it were worth it. Look 'ere.' He took his hand out of his pocket. In his grimy paw were five pennies.

Joe viewed this new-found wealth and asked, 'Go on then, clever dick, wheer'd tha get that?'

'Ah've been puttin' t'pig muck in a pile at t'side o' t'hut. Ah put it in me barrer an' selt it on t'allotments at a penny a bucket.' Joe chuckled.

'Well, ah've got ter 'and it ter thee son, th'art not daft. What tha gonna spend it on?'

Jimmy replied stoutly, 'Ah'm not spendin' it. It's goin' upstairs in me Oxo tin. Ah've got sempence in theer now. When ah put this in an' that thre'p'ny bit, ah'll 'ave one and three. If ah want owt fer t'pigs, it'll pay fer it.' Joe saw in his son a whole new light, respect dawning.

'Good fer thee, Jim. Ah think th'art goin' ter mek it. By t'end o' t'year tha'll be able ter start breeding.' Jim shook his head.

'Ah shan't Dad', he stated knowledgeably. 'Ralph says it'll be Feb'ry afore ah can breed, an' then it'll be sixteen weeks to 'em bein' born.'

His father remonstrated with him. 'What's this "Ralph" business? Ah think

26

yer mean Mester Meadows.'

'Oh it's awreight, Dad, 'e telled me ah could call 'im Ralph – we're big mates.' His chest swelled with pride. "E says my pigs is comin' on as good as 'is. 'E ast me if ah'd like ter go dahn an' 'ave a look at 'is termorrer.'

'Aye 'e's a good un is Ralph, an' just thee tek notice o' what 'e tells thee, tha wain't go far wrong.'

*   *   *

Bob Shaw, now supplied with an artificial leg by the War Office, had graduated to a walking stick and was in better spirits. Alice insisted on feeding him at every opportunity. Now and again he would help Jimmy out with the pigs, as he did on the day of the trip, and he helped him extend the hut with eggboxes from Hunter's. These were the boxes that the Egyptian eggs came in, about six feet long and ideal for the framework. The whole lot was covered in old linoleum.

The nights by now were getting cool and Jim decided that his charges would need more straw. He set off with his barrow one Saturday morning for the Oaks Farm, up near Bowden Houstead Wood. The farmer, Mr Bolsover, came to the door and stood gazing down, a tall, dour man, long-nosed and heavy-browed with grey sideburns and moustache.

'An' what can ah do for you, young man?' It was said in the tone of a busy man. Jim was not to be browbeaten.

'Ah've come ter buy some straw, Mester Bolsover.'

'Oh, tha wants a bit o' straw for thi rabbits, eh?'

'No, fer mi pigs. Ah'm goin' ter be breedin' 'em.'

Bolsover looked sceptical, but answered, 'Ah'll sell thee a bale, but it'll cost thee thre'pence.' Jim stuck his thumbs in an imaginary waistcoat.

'Tell yer what Mester Bolsover, ah'll gi'e yer sempence fer three bales.' Bolsover chuckled. 'Ah'll let yer 'ave 'em fer eightpence, it's best ah can do.'

Jimmy stuck out his hand. 'Done, Mester Bolsover.' The farmer gravely shook hands and as the lad fished in his pocket for the money, the farmer asked, 'Wheer's your place then lad?'

Jim answered, 'Mi piggery's just this side o' t'railway line at Darnall. They call me Jim Whiteley an' ah live on Kirby Road.' Holding out some coppers, he continued, 'Ah'll gi'e you fourpence now an' t'rest o' t'money when ah fetch t'last un.'

'Aye, that's awreight, Jim. Come on, ah'll show yer wheer t'straw is.' Bolsover glanced down as they crossed the yard. 'Aye, ah can see, tha's got pig muck on thi boots.'

Jim looked up and told the farmer, 'Ah got t'money fer t'straw sellin' pig muck.'

Bolsover roared with laughter and, putting his hand on Jim's shoulder, said,

'Tha'll do, Jim.' They loaded two bales onto the barrow and, with a wave to the farmer, Jim set off with his load.

On his return for the third bale, Jim knocked on the door of the farmhouse and Bolsover opened it.

''Ere y'are, Mester Bolsover, that fourpence I owe yer, an' thank you.'

'It's a pleasure, Jim. Any time ah can 'elp yer.' The lad asked, 'There is summat else. Ah leave school at Christmas an' ah'll be lookin' fer a job.'

Bolsover looked at him with respect. 'Ah'll keep thi in mind, lad. If ah've got owt ah'll let thi know.'

'Thank you very much. Tara', and he was away again. The farmer watched him go, pulling his bottom lip pensively.

★   ★   ★

Twice more Jimmy visited Oaks Farm for straw. In December, on the second trip, there had been a light fall of snow so he took his sledge. Arriving there, he resembled a snowman and as Mrs Bolsover opened the door, she burst out, 'You must be perished, Jimmy. Come in and I'll get you a cup o' tea.'

Then a thought occurred to her. 'Do you like stew?'

Jim nodded mutely, a little overawed at being invited in. When the woman asked if he'd like a bowl, he said eagerly, 'Yes please, Missis.'

The farmer's wife took one of his hands and inspected it. Seeing its condition, she remarked, 'I think you'd better wash these first, hadn't you?'

While she got the stew, Jim went to the sink and was still searching for the tap when Mrs Bolsover came over and showed him the hand-pump at the side. When she worked the handle the water that gushed out was icy, bone-achingly cold, as Jimmy scrubbed with the block of veined, blue and white washing soap. He wiped his hands on the old towel which hung on a nail and made his way to the table where a steaming bowl of stew awaited his attention. He was into his second slice of home-made bread when George Bolsover came in the back door.

He grinned across at his wife and remarked, 'That Jimmy knows his job. Ah see 'e's got 'is feet under t'table already, Ivy.'

'The lad was frozen when he got here', she retorted. 'He wanted somethin' warm inside him.'

The farmer, taking off his overcoat, answered, 'That's awreight, as long as 'e's left some for me.'

He was about to join Jim at the table when Ivy stopped him, saying, 'George Bolsover, get over there and wash your hands. I made Jimmy wash his.'

Bolsover grinned at the lad. 'She's a reight tartar, this missus o' mine', and he dutifully cleansed the offending members before joining Jimmy at the table. As they ate they talked about the animals, the farm and the weather. To the lad, George's words were pearls of wisdom to be saved and savoured. Their meal finished, they sat back with full stomachs. Ivy glanced meaningfully at her husband and asked, 'Didn't you say you'd have to go to Darnall today George?'

Getting the message, he turned to Jim, saying, 'Tell thee what, Jim, ah promised my mate ah'd see 'im in t' *Duke o' York*, ah could gi' yer a ride down. We could take yer straw down an' save yer some walkin'.' Jimmy was delighted.

'Thanks, Mester Bolsover, that'll be grand.' Then he stood up and dug in his pocket. ''Ere y'are, I owe yer eightpence.'

Now a Yorkshireman can be sentimental about many things. Mostly, he can be a good, loving husband and he's 'soft as barm' with kids and animals. However, when it comes to money, any man born under the White Rose becomes business-like. Accordingly, he accepted the money with the thought that the lad would be getting free transport. He slapped him on the back. 'Come on then, Jim, let's get that straw loaded.'

The big grey in the shafts, just out of a cold stable, was glad to be moving. Her step was high and her nostrils flared, breath pluming in the frosty air. Jimmy, standing beside George at the front of the cart, was really living, his dreams were coming true. George seemed to sense it, for he turned to his young friend, holding out the reins.

''Ere Jimmy, would yer like ter 'ave 'old?' Jim, his eyes saucers, stammered,

'I - I - I couldn't, Mester Bolsover, ah wouldn't know what to do.'

'It's easy lad, Bonnie's a good un', nodding at the horse, 'She answers well. 'Ere, get 'old o' t'reins wi' me. Nah, 'old 'er gently, she's got a soft mouth, that's it. If yer want 'er ter turn, just pull t'rein on that side. If yer want 'er ter stop, pull on both reins and shout "Whoa!". Theer y'are. See 'er ears turn, she knows we're talkin' abaht 'er.'

All too soon for Jimmy they were pulling up the lane beside the railway and past the paint factory. To Jimmy's unutterable delight, three of his friends were playing football on the waste ground and witnessed his triumphant arrival. As they reached the hut he shouted 'Whoa!' in as deep a voice as he could, leaned back on the reins and Bonnie immediately came to a stop right beside the hut.

The straw was unloaded and George climbed back into the cart. Then, with the reins in his hands, he turned to Jimmy.

'Look, son, Barry Wilson who delivers t'milk fer me's goin' in t'army in January. Ah wonder if yer'd like t'job.'

As Jim stood speechless, he continued, 'Tha'll 'ave ter be up early, we start at six an' tha'll be draggin' three churns on a barrer. Tha'll start on seven an' a tanner.'

Jimmy, at last finding his voice, burst out, 'It sounds awreight, Mester Bolsover'. Then, always cautious, 'But will ah 'ave ter pull t'barrer all t'way from t'farm?' George chuckled.

'No, Jim, ah'm not that bad. Ah'll bring t'milk down to your 'ouse an' pick up t'churns from t'day afore. An' be sure tha washes 'em aht well. Come an' see me on t'second o' January. So long', and the cart set off, to a casual wave from Jim.

Cockily, Jim swaggered across to his school friends, who were dumbfounded. Jack Alsop, the greengrocer's son, was the first to speak.

'Nah den, Jim, 'oo were that?'

Jim replied airily, 'Oh, he's just a mate o' mine. They call 'im Bolsover an' 'e's gorra farm.'

Weedy Stan Birtles, pushing up his glasses, asked, 'What were 'e sayin' ter thee, Jimmy?'

'Oh that. Well, after Christmas ah'm goin' ter work fer 'im. Ah'll be deliverin' your milk.' Reuben Greenwood, the third member, got Jim's barrow and pulled it round the hut, shouting 'Milko, Milko!' and it degenerated into a melée, the other two joining in.

Back at Kirby Road, Joan and Sally had the house to themselves and Sally was working on her face with oatmeal and milk while Joan was washing some underwear at the sink.

Joan asked, 'Where yer goin' tonight, Sal, anywhere nice?'

Sally, her face covered in oatmeal, replied, 'Ah'm goin' ter t'*Empire* ter see a variety. Will Fyffe's on an' that Chinese magician, Chung Ling Soo.'

Joan was silent as she got more water from the boiler in the Yorkshire range with the lading can. Over her shoulder she asked, 'Who're yer goin' with? As if ah didn't know.'

Sally flared up. 'Ah'm goin' wi' Bert Thompson, an' what about it?' She glared at the older girl's back, as if daring her to say something. Joan turned and sat down opposite her, her face concerned.

'Sal, yer know 'is reputation, everyone'll be talkin' about yer. Yer'll come 'ome wi' summat yer won't lose in a 'urry.' Sally's face was stubborn.

'It's nobody's business but mine. 'E's allus been a perfect gentleman'. Then her voice faltered. 'Except . . . 'e talks mucky, but it dun't mean owt. If 'e does try it on ah can 'andle 'im.' Joan sighed.

'I 'ope yer can, love, because yer know what mi dad'll do if 'e finds out.' She went back to the sink, while Sally went on with her cosmetic operation. Their mother, coming in with the shopping, sensed the atmosphere and glanced from one to the other.

''Ave you two been arguin' again?' Joan spoke up.

'It were nowt Mum. What yer got in t'package?' Alice's face was animated as she unwrapped it.

'Wait till yer see it. It's a dress. Ah got it off that table in t'back of 'Edge's, yer know – them unclaimed pledges.' She held the dress in front of herself. 'What do yer think?' Joan gazed at it critically.

'Ah like it, it suits yer. What do you think, Sally?'

30

'Ah think it's a bit owd-fashioned, they're not wearin' 'em like that now.' Joan laughed.

'Ooh, listen ter t'fashion model. 'Ow much did yer gi' 'em fer it?' Her mother giggled. 'Ah got it fer threepence.'

Joan answered, 'Yer got a bargain theer, Mum.' They went on unpacking the shopping as they gossiped about the local scandals.

At seven o'clock, as Joe and Alice were leaving for a drink at the *Bradley*, Bob Shaw came to the door.

"Ello Bob', said Joe. 'We're just goin' out, I 'ope Joan can keep yer entertained. We'll see yer later, and don't do anything ah wouldn't. That should gi' yer plenty ter do.' They left, leaving the couple to their own devices. The moment they were alone, Bob gave her his news.

'I got a letter today from t'War Office. They sent me forty-five pounds. 'Ow about that, love?' She threw her arms around him and kissed him.

'That's lovely, Bob, we can see about that shop now', and they went on talking, putting flesh on their dreams. Eight-thirty came and Jimmy came in, to be packed off to bed with two slices of bread and jam and a pot of cocoa. They listened to a record of John McCormack singing *Smiling Through* on the horn gramophone. Joan was winding it up to put on *Cavalliera Rusticana* when Sally came in. She was disturbed and her eyes were red and swollen. Bob looked from Sally to Joan and got up from his chair.

'Ah shan't be long, Joan, ah'll pop out an' fetch meself some fags', and he went out, leaving the two girls alone. Joan looked down at her sister, now a sorry figure, and said in a neutral tone, 'So it 'appened then, Sal?'

Sally's eyes were downcast, her colour high. 'Yes. 'E were as nice as pie first of all, then 'is arm come round me an' 'e were feelin' at me . . . me, top, yer know. Ah didn't stop 'im – 'e 'as spent a lot o' money on me – then before ah knew it 'is 'and were up mi frock'. She lifted her head. 'Ah couldn't believe it. 'E said "Come on darlin', yer know ah didn't bring yer out 'cos ah like yer face, it's time yer paid yer fare", an' all t'time 'is 'and were still gropin'.

"E treated me like a, like a . . .' Sally sobbed, unable to say the word. After a few seconds she choked out, 'T'bloke next door were smokin' a cigar so ah grabbed it and stuck it on Bert's cheek. 'E screamed and called me an effin' bitch an' ah dashed out an' come 'ome.' She put her head down and the tears ran unchecked. Joan put a comforting hand on her shoulder.

'Ne'er mind, Sal, it's over now. Just as long as yer've learnt summat. Wash yer face an' we'll go an' meet Bob in t'pub. Ah'll buy yer a gin.'

Joan and a chastened Sally walked into the smoke-laden snug of the *Bradley Well* and joined Bob, who was nursing a half of bitter.

Chapter Five

✦ ✦

ON CHRISTMAS MORNING Jim woke up early, while Tom, in the other bed, slumbered on. He lay there, his brain still drugged by sleep, then realised what day it was. Sitting up, he looked hopefully at the bottom of the bed and there was the pillow-slip. Reaching down, he pulled it to him, diving his hand in and finding a big box.

He pulled it out and discovered it to be a compendium of games. He opened the box, and feasted his eyes on the dominoes, draughts, and snakes and ladders. He fished in the sack again and found a flat object which turned out to be a torch that shone in three colours. Emptying the slip, there were the statutory apple and orange, accompanied by six brand new pennies. These went straight into his Oxo tin, making six-and-tuppence, painstakingly acquired over months.

As he experimented with the torch, Jim woke his brother, who investigated his own pillow-slip to find a new football and a jew's harp.

Joe was awakened by his sons playing football in the bedroom, and good humouredly shouted, 'Nah then, yer little sods, keep it quiet', then turned over and drifted once more into sleep beside Alice's warm body.

Jimmy was first up and about, to attend to his beloved pigs. Putting on an old overcoat that had been Sam's, he picked up the two buckets of swill that he'd been keeping on the still-warm hob. The fresh snow, as he stepped outside, was crisp with frost and crunched like candy as he blazed a trail towards the pigsty. He ducked through the railings and across the railway line, and was greeted ecstatically by his two charges, who by now weighed more than him. The boar, Punch, jostled him as he stepped into the run, and Jim lifted the bucket out of the pig's reach.

Judy, the sow, sniffed appreciatively at the other bucket as it steamed in the winter air. He had considered calling them Sally and Tom, but Alice had dissuaded him in the interests of family harmony.

'Be'ave yerselves', he chided, 'wait till ah gerrit in t'trough.' He emptied the unappetising mess into the home-made trough. By now he had extended his foraging to include the baker's, greengrocer's and butcher's, and anything was grist to his mill. Cabbage leaves, stale bread, potato peelings, in fact anything remotely edible was accepted by this budding tycoon.

While the pigs were feeding, Jim mucked out the hut and laid new straw. It was his constant fear that his animals would catch something if he didn't keep the sty clean; Ralph had told him harrowing tales of pigs slaughtered in their hundreds because of swine-fever.

The overcoat, sleeves turned back, flapped around his ankles as he clambered through the railings and made his way home, bent against the biting wind. As he reached the entry, he lifted his head and glanced down the street, eyes bleary with the cold. His heart leapt. There on the corner, by Appleton's chemist, was a familiar tall, khaki-clad figure.

'Sam, Sam', he yelled, dropping the buckets and running to meet his brother. The treacherous overcoat, wrapping round Jimmy's legs, sent him sprawling, but he scrambled up and ran on, in spite of skinned knees.

Together, the two brothers walked home, Jimmy babbling all the news – his dad's win, the pigs and what he'd got for Christmas, until they were turning into the entry.

Alice was poking life into the fire which had been banked up all night with ashes and wet tea leaves, when she heard the sneck go on the back door. Without looking round, she said, 'Come on an' get a warm, Jimmy, you must be perished.' As she turned she saw Sam standing there, kit-bag on shoulder. Her eyes brimmed.

'Hello, Mam', said Sam, taking off his peaked cap and revealing the army haircut. He came and put his arms around her, kissing her full on the mouth. She hugged him, then took his arms and held him away. She gazed at him searchingly.

'Yer lookin' well, son, ah think yer've put on a bit o' weight.' He grinned and joked,

'It's all that bully-beef and plum and apple jam.' Alice, with a feeling of disloyalty, couldn't help comparing this tall, healthy creature with the crippled, emaciated figure of Bob Shaw. It didn't seem fair, somehow, but another part of her rejoiced to have her son back, if only for a short while. She fussed about, putting on the kettle and warming the pot, as Sam sat down in Joe's chair, putteed legs thrust out.

The stairs door opened and Joe came down, grumbling. 'What's all t'row about? A bloke can't . . .' He saw Sam. At first he was tongue-tied, then blurted, 'Blimey, son, it's good ter see thee', and they embraced, slapping each other on the back. They sat down opposite each other and Joe asked the eternal question.

'When yer goin' back, Sam?'

His son answered, joking. 'I've only just got 'ere', he laughed, 'I've only got seven days, but I'll pinch New Year's Eve.'

'Yer couldn'ter timed it better.' Joe passed Sam a Woodbine. 'Did yer see much action?'

'No, not a lot, I was only in t'front line for about a week, then I went over the top and got shot in the foot. I wangled myself a soft job in t'quarter-master's stores. I even got promoted.' He pointed to his sleeve with its corporal's stripes.

'Well, yer did yer bit, so there's no shame in that.' Father and son chatted as they drank tea out of big, pint mugs, while Tom and Jimmy hovered on the fringes. Sally and Joan came down and there was another reunion. Joe shouted over the hubbub. 'Look, everybody, get ready an' we'll go to t'*Bradley* an' celebrate. It's not often yer son comes 'ome a hero.' Alice demurred,

'If yer don't mind, Joe, me an' Joan'll stop an' get t'dinner ready. Just bring us one back.' Sally said the same and Alice thanked her with her eyes.

While Joe was getting ready, Sam turned to the two lads, handing them each half-a-crown – half a year's spending money.

'Here y'are, kids, buy yourselves a sarsaparilla at Elliot's.' With effusive thanks, the two boys dashed off to spend their new-found wealth.

★　　★　　★

In the pub it was celebration time for the returning hero, and the pints flew thick and fast. Little Harry Benson on the piano struck up with *Keep the Home Fires Burning,* and all the pub joined in. At half-past-one, when Sam was into his seventh pint, he saw Bob Shaw come in and waved him over. Sam leaned over the bar and ordered a pint and as Nobby pulled it he reached into his pocket and pulled out a roll of notes.

His father, standing beside him, remarked, 'Yer didn't get that sort o' money on a shilling a day.'

Sam laughed uncertainly and replied, 'Well, I had a couple of sidelines goin' with bein' in the stores.' He picked up his pint and took it across to Bob, who'd found himself a seat. He sat down on the next stool and Bob said, 'Ted o'er theer tells me yer were injured in action. Wheer were yer injured?'

Sam leaned over and confided, the beer loosening his tongue, 'Between you and me, Bob, I shot missen in the foot. I wasn't stayin' in the front line.' He laughed. 'A man could get killed.'

Bob stared at him coldly, then stood up, leaning on his stick. Without a word, he picked up the pint that Sam had bought and carefully poured it in the soldier's lap. He limped out, his face graven stone.

Joe saw Bob leave, and as Sam returned to the bar, greatcoat over the wet uniform, he asked, 'What's up wi' Bob? 'E didn't stop long.'

'He wasn't feelin' very well', Sam replied. 'He's gone home', and he joined in with the singing.

★　　★　　★

Alice was at the sink peeling potatoes, and Joan was podding the peas while Sally laid the table. The two girls were chattering amongst themselves, but their mother was silent, absorbed in her own thoughts. She put the potatoes on to boil in the big, cast-iron saucepan then, facing her daughters with a concerned expression mused, 'Y'know, I might be funny, but that's not *our* Sam that's come back from France. 'E's a different lad now. Summat's 'appened ter

34

change 'im.'

''E's learnt ter stand on 'is own feet', suggested Sally, putting her hand on her mother's shoulder. ''E's not a mummy's boy anymore.'

Joan disagreed. 'No, Sal, it's not that. It's summat in 'is eyes. When 'e's talkin' ter yer, 'is eyes are lookin' behind yer.' Alice agreed.

'That's it, Joan. I 'ate ter say it about me own son, but 'e looks sly. Ah keep gettin' t'feelin' 'e's lyin', an' that's summat 'e never did ter me.' The conversation languished as they all busied themselves with the dinner.

When Joe and Sam returned from the pub they were distinctly merry and carried three bottles of brown ale. They took off their coats and were about to sit down when Sam exclaimed, 'Hey, I forgot. Where's my kit-bag?'

He went over, unlaced the bag and plunged his hand in. He felt around and pulled out two tissue-wrapped packets, ceremonially handing one to each parent. Alice unwrapped hers first, and as she removed the final layer of paper she gasped and stopped breathing for long, uncounted seconds.

There on the tissue lay a cross on a silver chain, a full two-and-a-half inches in length, blazing with diamonds and sapphires in the slant of winter sun that speared through the window. Even to Alice's unsophisticated eyes it shouted of the kind of quality you'd be hard put to find in H.L. Brown's the jeweller's, which was her only yardstick of excellence.

While she stood mesmerised, Joe unwrapped his present and found himself holding a watch, heavy with red gold and hung from an ornate chain. Opening the front, he found the hours marked with tiny diamonds. As one, they held the gifts out to each other, wordlessly, then withdrew them to gaze again with eyes of wonder. Alice was the first to break the spell.

'I can't tek this Sam, it's too much. It must 'ave cost . . .' Her brain refused to compute the value. Joe joked to cover his dilemma.

'No, son, ter wear that ah'd 'ave ter buy missen a boozer.' Sam went to his mother and took the crucifix, placing the chain around her neck.

'Nothing's too good for my mam an' dad. I bought 'em specially.' She studied her son as he fastened the clasp, but once again, his eyes didn't meet hers. Deep inside her a worm of doubt began gnawing, but she kissed and thanked him. Joe shook him by the hand. 'Thanks, son, it's summat ah've allus wanted.'

The Christmas dinner went ahead with a festive leg of pork – chicken or turkey being much too expensive. Afterwards, the men retired to bed to sleep off the beer, ready for the evening. Alice and the girls set to, clearing the wreckage, but not before the silver cross had been enviously examined.

⋆   ⋆   ⋆

Seven o'clock on the dot, the whole family except for Tom and Jimmy walked into the 'best room' at the *Bradley*, all primed for a big night. They annexed a table and proceeded to lay the foundation for a Boxing Day hangover. The beer flowed freely on this big night of the year, and even Nobby the landlord had donned a collar and tie in honour of the occasion. At nine o'clock, however, Joan asked to be excused.

'I told Bob ah'd pop in – 'e's spending tonight at 'ome with 'is mam an' dad. Ah'll see yer back at 'ome. Merry Christmas.' She walked out, leaving them to their celebrations.

As she entered Bob's house, his father welcomed Joan with a glass of port and showed her to a seat next to her fiancé. Bob seemed strangely subdued. They talked with Jack and Connie about the future shop, but all the time Joan kept glancing at Bob, unable to understand what was troubling him. At half-past- ten the little, bird-like Connie got up and made cocoa for everybody. She and Jack took theirs to bed, for as he explained, 'Ah'm goin' on t'market in t'morning, ah might mek a few bob.'

They retired, and Joan sipped at the scalding cocoa, then turned to the brooding Bob. 'Come on, Bob, what's a matter wi' yer? There's summat gettin' up yer nose, love.'

Bob sat in thought for a moment, then explained, hesitantly, 'This dinner, ah poured a pint over Sam in t'*Bradley*.'

Joan giggled. 'Yer mean yer spilt yer beer down 'im?'

'No. Ah did it on purpose. 'E told me 'e'd shot 'isself in t'foot ter keep out o' t'front line. Ah'm sorry, Joan, ah just couldn't 'elp it.' Absently, he scratched the knee of his metal leg. Joan, looking straight ahead, spoke in a tight, controlled voice.

'Don't blame yerself, Bob, yer did quite right.' She faced him, pent-up fury in her eyes. 'Do you mind if I go 'ome, Bob? Ah've got summat ter say ter that heroic brother o' mine.' He tried to calm her down, but she was adamant.

When he offered to come with her, she answered, 'All right, but this is between me an' 'im.' Reluctantly, he went with her, kicking himself for his big mouth.

At the Whiteley residence, Alice was getting the supper. Joe, sitting in the chair, took the gold timepiece from his waistcoat pocket. In a voice slurred by drink, he remarked to no-one in particular, 'Ah'd better wind me new watch.'

He stood and reached onto the high mantelpiece for his watch-key. Putting on his spectacles, he opened the back of the watch, then stopped and tried to read the inscription.

'Hey, Sam, what's this say? Ah think it's in French.' His son came and glanced at the letters engraved there.

'Oh, that's the name o' the maker, "*Jean Leroux*", and 1875 is when the firm started.'

As they stood looking at the watch, the door opened and Joan came in, eyes blazing. She faced her brother and asked him, 'Is it true what ah've 'eard? That my brave brother', she spat out the words, 'shot 'isself in t'foot so 'e wouldn't

36

'ave ter feight?'

Shamefaced, Sam said nervously, 'I wasn't t'on'y one, a lot more did it.'

His father, face stormy, rumbled, 'On'y bleedin' cowards did it.' The watch was open in his hand and he held it out to Bob, without taking his furious eyes from his son.

'What's it say on this watch, Bob? Ah can't read it, it's in French.' Bob took the watch and read it, haltingly.

'*To Jean Leroux . . . on 'is twenty-first birthday . . . from 'is father. . . in 1875.*' Then, almost whispered, '*with all my love*'. The words dropped like stones into the silence.

Joe, his voice deceptively quiet, asked, 'Tell me, Sam, 'ow do yer come ter 'ave an old man's watch?'

His son laughed weakly, 'Oh, you know these froggie peasants, they'll give yer anything for a few tins o' bully and some biscuits.'

Joe's face suffused with blood and he roared, 'So, th'art a con man as well as a coward.' His big, calloused hands worked, seeking something to tear. 'Are tha a bloody thief an' all? Who did tha pinch that money off that's in thi pocket – some poor widder?'

Sam backed away in fear; this was a man that he'd never seen. As he turned to flee, one big hand grabbed his collar, then his trousers tightened in his crotch as he was lifted off his feet. He was frog-marched to the door, then pitched bodily into the yard, his face hitting the scullery wall as he flew sprawling into the snow. Stunned, he scrambled to his feet, blood running down his face, and looked up at the avenging figure of his father.

He faltered, almost pleading, 'But, Dad, you can't do this, I'm yer son'.

'Th'art not mi bloody son, th'art a bastard. Nah get, afore ah kill thee.' The door slammed, to open again as his kit-bag came flying out, knocking him down once more. The family stood transfixed as Joe emerged from the darkness of the scullery, and it was an old man that walked in and slumped in the chair, all anger drained from him.

Head in trembling hands, he whispered brokenly, 'What did ah do wrong? What did ah do?'

Alice was the first to move. She put a comforting hand on his shoulder. 'Tha didn't do owt wrong, Joe, 'e were just a bad un.'

It was nearly a relief to her, as the worm of doubt within her rested and she realised that she had nurtured it for many years. Her mind went back to the milk money that sometimes went missing, Joe's fags that she'd had to replace, and the precious pennies lost from her purse. The pain was still there, but now it wasn't doubt, it was the certainty that hurt. She pushed it to the back of her mind – it was her man that mattered now.

Joan came and handed her father a pot of tea and he took it automatically with a, 'Thanks lass', then drank, holding it in both hands as he stared into the fire. Alice bent, and murmured to him.

'Yer've still got two sons, Joe, an' they're good uns.'

'Aye, th'art reight, Mother', he said, and putting the pot on the table, beckoned the two lads who still stood, unsure. They came and stood in front of him and he gazed at them for a moment, then said, 'Look, ah'm no angel, an' ah know bloody well you're not – no lad is that's wuth owt – but whatever you do, 'owever bad it is, come an' tell me abaht it. Don't ever lie ter me, 'cos if yer do, yer'll get t'same as . . .' He couldn't say the name and ended, cocking his thumb, 'Same as 'e got. Awreight?'

They nodded mutely, impressed by this speech from their father, who wasn't renowned for his oratory. Accepting a cup of cocoa each, they disappeared upstairs to talk long into the night. Bob limped across and handed Joe the watch that he was still holding gingerly, as if it was explosive, and told his future father-in-law, 'Sorry, Mister Whiteley, I 'ope yer won't 'old it against me.'

The older man gave a tired smile and answered, 'No, it were no fault o' thine, son.' He got to his feet, holding out his hand. 'Merry Christmas, Bob, an' I 'ope ah see yer in t'*Bradley* termorrer.'

Joan went to see Bob out, while Sally kissed her father and took her cup of cocoa to bed. Joan did likewise and murmured, ''Night, Dad, don't let it get yer down, there's plenty on us left.'

When they were alone, Alice took off the cross, gazed at it wistfully and handed it to Joe, asking, 'What're we goin' ter do wi' 'em, Joe?'

Her husband sat and looked at the jewellry, his thoughts his own, and replied, 'Ah don't know, love, but ah'm certain we can't use 'em. Ah'll leave it ter thee, lass.'

He lifted his head and continued, 'For all we know, t'people that own 'em could be dead now, an' there'd be no way of findin' 'em any'ow. Ah think we'll put 'em away while we mek us mind up.

The treasure was rewrapped and placed in the old handbag, along with Alice's engagement ring and Joe's best cufflinks. The peace of Christmas descended on Kirby Road.

★   ★   ★

Boxing day passed, accompanied by the intake of enormous amounts of Stones' best bitter, followed by a repeat on New Year's Eve. Once again, the high time of the year was over and the Whiteleys were back to the serious business of living, or, as some would say, existing.

By today's standards, their life was barren, and small pleasures took on the status of much more sophisticated enjoyment. On the terminus there were no Joneses to keep up with – everyone was in the same precarious boat, often kept afloat by people who were in the same position as those they aided. Consequently, anyone making an outward show of wealth was no longer a member of the club and would have to plough a lonely furrow.

Jimmy was up at seven o'clock on January 2nd, after an early night, and he was off through the snow with his buckets of swill. By now, the two big pink pigs had become part of his life, but he knew that if he got his milk round he would have to make other arrangements. He pushed his way into the sty as Punch and Judy jostled him – over six hundred pounds of prime pork.

'Mek t'best orrit you two, 'cos yer goin' ter get it at teatime if ah get that job. Punch, gi' Judy a chance, yer greedy owd bugger.' He glanced around guiltily to see if anyone was listening. Each morning, alone with his two friends, he would tell them his secrets, his hopes and his fears, and they replied with suitable grunts and squeals.

The chill was beginning to bite, so he fastened the gate and headed for home. As he pushed his way through the iron railings, the thought crossed his mind that he wouldn't be able to use this route for much longer. He was now four-foot-ten and nearly nine stone and looked set to emulate his father's stocky build. His hair, covered now by a balaclava, was an unruly chestnut-brown that refused to take a parting. Below it were features that would become rugged, given time, and a firm jaw. It was the face of a rebel.

After his usual breakfast of porridge with bread and dripping, Jimmy was on his way to Manor Farm for his date with destiny – his first job. Inside, he was quaking. It was the biggest step of his short life, his entry into the world of men. Trudging through the thick snow, he thought back to the familiar schoolroom that he had so recently quitted. He realised now, too late, that he had enjoyed learning and he felt cheated. Deep down he knew he wasn't ready to take on the responsibility of his own fate.

When he reached the farmhouse, he stopped ten yards from the door. He gathered his reserves, then stepped forward and knocked, taking off his balaclava. He was about to knock again when a voice shouted, 'Mornin, Jim, ah've been expectin' thee.' It was George Bolsover emerging from the cowshed.

'Mornin', Mester Bolsover. Ah thought ah'd come an' 'ave a word.'

'Glad yer came, Jim, ah'd like yer ter start a' Monday if yer can.'

'Awreight, Mester Bolsover, ah'll be ready.' He held out his hand. Bolsover shook it, saying,

'Good lad – an' forget the "Mester", yer'd best call me George if we're goin' ter work together. Come in an' 'ave a cup o' tea while we talk about it.' The farmer's wife was filling the teapot as they came through the door, and remarked, 'Yer must 'ave smelt it, ah've just mashed.' They sat down at the table; George rubbed his chin.

'Ah've been thinking, Jim. Bein' as yer live up Kirby Road, ah think yer could start at half-past-six. Yer do Kirby Road first, Station Road, Owler Greave an' then cross over for t'others. Ah've written it all down. Yer'll finish at Whitby Road School – t'teachers tek abaht three pints.' He got up, went to the sink and came back with three measures made of shiny metal, with brass labels. They had hooked handles to hang on the churn's edge.

'These are your measures, Jim, quart, pint an' gill. Gi' 'em a good shout when yer comin' up t'street, an' don't miss anybody, but mek sure yer get t'money. Ah'll pick it up when ah bring t'milk.'

Jim sipped the thick, sweet tea and asked, 'Would yer mind, Mest . . . George, if ah pick up me swill on t'round?'

The farmer chuckled and said to his wife, ''E doesn't miss a trick, does 'e, Ivy?' Then, to Jim, 'Course tha can, lad, it's thee that's pullin' t'barrer, an' if there's any milk left, tha can gi' it ter t'pigs, it wain't keep while mornin'.'

'Oh, ta . . . George, that'll be 'andy.' Jim rose to his feet. 'Anyway, ah'll 'ave ter get off nah, ah've got ter get mi barrer ready, ah'll see yer.'

As he made for Darnall to tell Punch and Judy, he didn't notice the driving snow, for he was walking a foot above the ground. Trudging across the fields, his hands thrust into the pockets of the hand-me-down overcoat, Jim saw himself with his own farm and hundreds of pigs and cows. He'd got nearly ten shillings in the Oxo tin, and now he was a working man there was no limit.

After he'd told the pigs – who both registered their approval – he continued on home to inform his mother that she would be a few bob better off. Hands in trouser pockets, he was pointedly casual.

''Ow much do yer think ah'll get outa mi wages then, Mam? Ah'll be gerrin' seven an' a tanner.' Alice smiled.

'Ah think yer'll be able ter keep ninepence a week.' His face lit up and he threw his arms around her.

'Ta, Mam, that'll be great.' She carried on cleaning, then turned to him.

'Ah forgot, Jim, you 'aven't 'eard. Joan an' Bob are gettin' married next month an' they want you ter be groomsman. They've got chance of a shop down Shirland Lane at five bob a week, an' they on'y want twenty-five pounds for t'stock.'

Jim, sitting in his father's chair, asked, 'What's a groomsman do, Mam?'

'A groomsman 'as to see that the groom's prop'ly dressed an' that.'

'Do I 'ave ter mek a speech?'

'No, that's t'best man's job. Tom's t'best man, an' 'e's not lookin' forrard to it.' She rambled on, glad of the company, while Jimmy dreamed.

★   ★   ★

On Saturday, Jim, in honour of his new employment, got a sugar box and built himself a new barrow. He decided after much heart-searching that his old one, steeped in pig manure, was hardly suitable for milk deliveries. He had scrounged two old cast-iron mangle wheels to take the weight of three churns. He was quite proud of it. It had a leg at one end for when he stopped to serve customers, and the shafts were joined with an old leather belt so that he could pull the weight up the hills.   As a final touch, he painted MILK on the sides. It was the talk of the street when he parked it outside the front door.

At half-past-seven Jim's father returned from town, and as he came in he threw a parcel to the lad. Excitedly, Jim undid the string (which his mother thriftily rolled up and put in the drawer). and removed the brown paper. His delighted eyes beheld . . . his first long trousers. Not only that, but they were moleskins, like his dad's. He jumped up.

'Ta, Dad, they're lovely.' Jim held them against himself. Joe watched him and grinned, 'If yer gonna be a workin' man, yer want t'reight clo'es. They'll last fer years.' Jim dashed upstairs to try on his new acquisition, the symbol of reaching his little majority. He was back in a short while, his walk stiff and artificial. For the first time in his life his legs were covered and, truth to tell, it felt strange and uncomfortable.

Lookin down, he said to his mother, 'They're a bit long, Mam, can yer shorten 'em?' Alice eyed the trousers, concertina'd round his ankles, and tried not to laugh.

'Yes, ah'll shorten 'em fer yer, then we can let 'em down as yer grow. Tek 'em off an' ah'll do 'em.'

Jim demurred, 'No, leave 'em fer just now. Can't we tuck 'em up fer t'time bein'?' The 'long uns' were duly pinned up and Jim went off to show his mates. He knew they'd be hanging about near the 'Iron Duke'.

Arriving at this Victorian monument to personal hygene – whose clients were visible from the top deck of passing trams – he found Jack and Reuben sharing a ha'p'orth of chips. As they watched him approach with awe, Jack remarked, 'Ah like thi keks, Jim. Wheer did tha gerrem?'

'Oh, mi dad fetched 'em from town. Ah start work on Monday, tha knows. 'As tha seen mi new barrer?' Reuben, who had been trying to climb the gaslamp, asked, 'What were wrong wi' thi owd un?'

'Tha what? Ah couldn't use that fer t'milk, it stinks rotten o' pigshit. Ah'd be awreight wi' t'customers comin' fer t'milk 'owdin' ther noses, wun't ah?'

Jack chuckled. 'Owd lass Foster wun't notice, their 'ouse smells worse than thy pigsty.'

Reuben, halfway up the gaslamp, shouted, 'Ah don't know abaht *their* 'ouse, *she* does. Ah got be'ind 'er in t'chipshop t'other day. Ah thought t'fish 'ad gone rotten.' They all laughed.

Jack Alsop delved in his pocket and came up with a battered cigarette. He struck a match on the 'Iron Duke' after three unsuccessful attempts on the seat of his pants. Puffing smoke with a great show of enjoyment, he offered it to Jim, the end wet with saliva.

''Ere, want a drag?' Jimmy declined.

'No bloody fear, Jack, ah've seen me father in a mornin', coughin' 'is 'ead off.

Th'art not gettin' me on that game.' He peered into the paper that Jack held. 'Gi' us a chip then, yer mingy sod.'

It was barely light as Jim dragged himself out of bed on his first working morning. At six-fifteen he was peering through the parlour window, watching for George bringing the milk. The new barrow was parked outside the entry. As the grey trotted up the street with George, he dashed out and met it at the kerb.

'Mornin', George. Cowd, innit?' The farmer tied the reins and stepped down, boots crunching in the snow like it was white meringue.

'It's perishin', lad.' He and Jim swung the first churn into the barrow. 'Ah don't envy yer in this lot, mate.'

They lifted another shining churn and Jim replied, 'That's awreight, George, ah'm used to it.' The last one was loaded. 'Ah'm aht at this time ter feed t'pigs most mornin's.' Bolsover leaned into the cart.

''Ere, Jim, ther's yer money-bag. Ther's five bob in change, so tek that aht before yer gi' me t'money termorrer. He turned the cart and made for home. As he reached the main road he heard the cry of 'Milko' echoing in the frosty air. He nodded and smiled to himself as he clicked his tongue at Bonny.

Throughout the day as he poured the milk, frothing, into the jugs brought out by the customers Jim practised his barrowside manner. His opening gambit was 'Cowd innit missis?', and he received such answers as 'Aye, it plays 'ell wi' mi screws', or 'Yer must be perished son'. Old Mrs Bowskill on Irving Street came back out with a pair of gloves.

''Ere, put these on, my 'Erbert wain't be needin' 'em wheer 'e's gone.'

By the time he reached Whitby Road, Jim felt he'd never been so tired in his life, and he'd never been so glad to see Kirby Road. He took the barrow into the yard, then went to his mother.

'Do yer want any milk, Mam? Ah've got some left.' Alice looked doubtful.

'Ah don't want any if it's goin' ter get yer in trouble.'

'No, it's awreight. George said ah could 'ave what's left if ther weren't a lot.' Then, magnanimously, he added, 'Ah think ah can let yer 'ave two pints'. His mother was ecstatic.

'Ah'll pop down ter Hunter's an' get some rice, we'll 'ave a milk puddin'.'
While she was gone, Jim left two pints in the jug and took the rest with the
swill to feed Punch and Judy, who thought it was their birthday.

★   ★   ★

Through the weeks that followed, as the takings on the round rose, George
Bolsover realised that Jim was a real asset. Occasionally, the farmer let him
drive the horse on trips round Darnall after the milkround. It was balm to his
soul as he swept up the terminus to see the envious eyes of his mates.

One day, he was stabling Bonny after one of these trips, and the grey was
nuzzling him for a carrot that he'd saved from his swill, George remarked, 'You
an' Bonny get on like an 'ouse on fire, don't yer?'

Jim, stroking the long neck, still rough with it's winter coat, replied, 'Aye,
we're t'best o' mates. She knows every word ah say, don't yer Bonny?' The
mare investigated his pocket in the hope of more titbits. Bolsover stood over
and watched him, deep in thought, then asked, 'It's your sister's wedding on
Sat'day, innit?'

The lad turned to face him and the mare nudged him between the shoulder
blades. 'Gi' o'er, Bonny.' Then, to George, 'Aye, it is. Ah'm t'groomsman.'

''Ow's she gettin' to t'church?'

'She's walkin' – it's on'y round t'corner an' she's not crippled.' George went
on, 'Do yer think she'd like ter ride theer?'

'Aye, but it's 'ardly worth catchin' t'tram, it's on'y one stop.'

The farmer beckoned mysteriously and Jim followed him towards a shed on
the far side of the house. George flung the doors wide, and when Jim eventually
found his voice, he blurted 'Why, it's beautiful Mester Bolsover. Ah've never
seen owt like it. It's . . . marvellous!'

There in the shed, bright in its livery of red, green and gold, was a gig with
tall, slim-spoked wheels, its harness silver with shiny black leather. Like a
sleepwalker, Jim went over and stroked the glossy paintwork. George grinned
indulgently. ''Ow'd yer like ter drive Joan ter church in that?'

Jim stared, unbelieving. 'Do yer mean it, George? Could ah?'

''Course yer can, Jim, yer've done some bloody good work fer me. Yer know
'ow ter use t'whip, don't yer?'

The lad spun round, indignant. 'Ah'd never use t'whip on Bonny.'

Bolsover laughed. 'No, ah don't mean that, ah mean when yer signal what
yer goin' ter do.'

'Oh, ah know that – an' ah'll be reight careful wi' it.'

'Right then, yer can pick it up early Sat'day morning.' After a hasty goodbye,
Jim went off to break the news to his sister.

43

O N THE MORNING of the wedding, Jimmy was attending to his charges. Judy by now was quite fat. 'Yer gerrin' big, girl. It won't be long now afore yer've gorra family, 'ey?' He went back to the house for a quick change and then he was on his way for the gig. He was at the farm by eight o'clock, face glowing with the bite of the wind. George greeted him.

'Hello lad, yer come fer t'gig?'

'Aye, I 'ave please, but . . . could ah groom Bonny afore ah tek 'er? Ah'd like 'er ter look good.'

For half-an-hour he curried and brushed Bonny until she was sleek and glossy – most of her winter coat was gone. Lovingly, he buckled her into the shafts of the shining gig. Ivy came out and tied a red ribbon in the mare's forelock, as she stamped to be off. Holding the reins, Jim looked down at George and his wife and stammered, 'Ah - ah can't ever thank yer enough Mester Bolsover.' 'George' wasn't good enough for the owner of this magnificent vehicle.

'Ah'll see yer abaht three o'clock. So long.' He shook the reins and Bonny high-stepped out of the yard, proud as a strutting bantam.

Pulling in from the main road, he spied his father, dressed in his best, talking to a neighbour at the top of the entry. The showman in him made him take a tight turn in front of the house to bring Bonny in with a flourish, right opposite the front door. He tied off the reins at the front of the gig, went round to the horse and said, 'Good lass, Bonny'. She whickered softly as he stroked her cheek.

He headed for the entry and greeted his audience with, 'Hallo, Dad, Mester Watson', and disappeared down the passage. Two pairs of approving eyes watched him go.

Joe and Tom set off for the church at a quarter-to-two. Ten minutes later the front door opened and Jim came out to stand behind the vehicle. Seconds later Joan came out, looking lovely in the beautiful old wedding dress in écru lace with matching veil. She was followed by Sally, and Norah, a neighbour's girl, who were the bridesmaids. Jim gallantly handed them into the gig, then boarded it himself.

Joan whispered, 'Thanks ever so much, Jim, yer a brick. It's beautiful.' He held the grey to a sedate trot and, with a clear road, took a smooth turn towards the terminus. There, half the population of Darnall seemed to be waiting.

The gig made a wide, sweeping curve around the 'Iron Duke', and Jim gave a quiet 'Whoa!' into Bonny's flicked-back ears and leaned back on the reins. The gig rolled to a gentle stop at the church door. As he climbed down, Jim saw a face in the crowd. It was a smiling George who gave the boy a thumbs-up which made his day. His shoulders squared and he proudly handed down his passengers.

As Joan entered the church on her father's arm, Jim buttonholed a younger boy he knew. Handing him a penny, he commanded,

''Ere, look after the gig while we come out, an' there'll be another penny fer yer.' He strode nonchalantly into the church.

The wedding went like well-oiled clockwork. Bob negotiated the aisle with scarcely a limp and the radiant bride came out on the arm of her new husband midst a blizzard of confetti. A proud Jimmy ferried them down to the *Bradley* for the 'do', after first rewarding his minder with the promised penny.

As the bride swept into the pub, George strolled down with Ivy on his arm and greeted Jim. 'Tha did a grand job, lad. Ah couldn't 'a done better missen. Thee an' Bonny mek a great pair. From now on tha'd better use Bonny on thi round. T'way it's pickin' up, tha'll need another churn, an' tha can't pull four in thi barrer.' Jim's tongue stumbled as he thanked his boss, but George cut him short.

'Awreight, Jim, thee get in an' enjoy thissen. Me an' Ivy'll tek Bonny 'ome. Come up an' fetch 'er in t'mornin'. So long, son.' The mare was away at a canter.

★ ★ ★

Jim, by now over five-feet tall, had become a well-known figure around Darnall with the horse and cart. He could still collect his swill after he'd done his round, which was fortunate, for at the end of March he went one day to the sty to be greeted only by Punch. Puzzled, he stepped into the hut. Judy lay there, suckling eight small, pink piglets. She looked up apologetically as Jim bent down and scratched her behind the ears.

'Tha's done a good job, Judy. They're beautiful, aren't they, lass? Ah'll 'ave ter pop round and see Ralph about yer.' Leaving Judy's swill in the hut, he closed the door to keep the proud father out of the way, then went to tell his parents the good news.

Joe exclaimed, 'That's great, Jim, an' all credit due ter thee. Tha's 'ad more patience than ah would 'ave, ah'll tell thee. What tha gonna do, sell 'em?'

Jim pursed his lips, then answered, 'Ah've been thinkin' abaht that, Dad. What ah'll do, ah'll sell Punch nah, an' keep Judy while she's finished sucklin' t'young uns. Then it'll depend whether ah can get a proper place. Ah might breed off 'er again or ah might sell 'er for pork.'

He broke off as Joe had another of the coughing fits that had been occurring more and more frequently of late. Alice was worried. 'Yer'll 'ave ter get off ter t'doctor's, Joe, th'art not gettin' any better.'

Joe wiped his lips with his handkerchief and answered testily, 'Don't wittle, woman. It's on'y wi' t'smokin', ah'll cut 'em dahn a bit.'

Jim was concerned. 'Ah think she's reight, Dad. That cough's awful. Yer'll 'ave ter gerrit seen to.'

Joe picked up his paper. 'That's enough from thee, young un, ah'll go when ah'm good an' ready.' It was the final word. Jim shrugged his shoulders and went off to High Hazels Bottom in search of Ralph Meadows.

The big, bluff pigman was sitting on the wall of his sty, smoking a pipe. He watched Jim as he came down the lane, then took his pipe out of his mouth.

"Ello Jim, what can ah do fer yer?' The youth sat down beside him.

'Ah thought yer'd like ter know, she's pigged last night, eight good uns, an' ah want some advice.'

'Glad t'ear it, lad.' He got to his feet. 'Ah'll come up an' take a look at 'em.' They strolled up the lane companionably.

Ralph squatted down and studied the eight newcomers, all once again imbibing nourishment. He picked one up and gave Jim a word of warning.

'Watch this one, ah think 'e'll be t'recklin'. Gi' it a couple o' weeks, an' if 'e isn't puttin' on weight, yer want ter knock 'im in t'ead, 'cos 'e'll never mek owt. Ah know it sounds cruel, but it's no good keepin' a bad un. But t'others are in good fettle.'

'I expected ter lose one or two, Ralph. By the way, while yer 'ere, what d'yer think that beggar outside weighs? Ah'm thinkin' o' sellin' 'im.' Ralph stepped outside and looked Punch over.

'Ah'd say 'e'd mek up three 'undred pound, Jim. Tell yer what, when yer ready, bring 'im dahn ter my place. Ah've got a balance theer, ah'll weigh 'im fer yer, then yer can tek 'im ter Armitage's, 'e's a good porker.'

'Thanks, Ralph, it's good o' yer ter tek t'trouble.'

'It's nowt, Jim, just let me know when yer comin'. Ah'll 'ave ter gerroff nah, so ah'll see yer later.'

He started off, but then turned back. 'Yer know what we were sayin' abaht another sty?' Jim nodded. 'Against my place there's an empty set o' sties. Ah think t'lad 'at 'ad 'em went into t'army. Ah'll see if ah can find aht abaht 'em, yer might get 'em fer a bob a week, an' it'd be big enough fer what you want.'

★   ★   ★

Each week Jim had a day off, either Wednesday or Thursday, to compensate for the fact that he delivered milk on both Saturdays and Sundays, but on his days off all his mates were either working or at school.

Unnoticed by him, he was fast becoming a loner, quite happy with his own company. His contemporaries were drifting into ruts carved by previous generations, but Jim had his own, as yet half-formed, ideas that there were other roads to travel.

As the trees began to turn green, Jim started going for long walks in the surrounding countryside. One fine spring day he hiked over to the uplands at Hyde Park. Purely by chance he had chosen one of the best vantage points from which to see his city. Disappointment awaited him. He was standing in bright sunlight, yet below him, where there should have been a panorama of this great city of steel, all that could be seen was a thick pall of smoke. In places, it was a devil's rainbow – virulent green, sulphurous yellow or glaring orange – depending on which poison each chimney was spewing out over acre upon acre of mean dwellings.

Though only fourteen, Jim could comprehend what this muck must be doing to the people below. He said to himself, 'Aye, Father, that's what's wrong wi' yer chest'. And he understood why it was always so much brighter up on the hills.

There was one other memorable day that was to have a profound effect on Jim's outlook and future. He had taken a parcel of sandwiches and a bottle of cold tea and headed south through Bowden Houstead Wood. This was a huge area of woodland, as yet unspoiled, and still populated by squirrels, foxes and rabbits. He wandered on, under the old, old trees, now breaking into leaf, much farther than he'd ever ventured before. Looking back through a gap in the trees, he could see in the distance the spire of Darnall Church, with the buildings huddled round, as if for warmth.

The sun was high and he was in a virgin part of the woodland. Pushing his way through some bushes, he stopped and gazed in astonishment. In the heart of the wood, like an oasis in a desert, was a garden with rows of vegetables, flowers and fruit bushes. At one end of the clearing was a cabin, built of wood, and from the chimney, smoke was ascending, blue, into the still air.

Rooted there, he recalled the legends told at school of an old hermit in the deep reaches of this miniature Sherwood. The stories portrayed this recluse as a wizard. In spite of himself, a shadow of fear invaded his mind. The door of the cabin opened, and a tall, spare man with a shock of long grey hair emerged. He stood, eyes shaded, gazing across at his young visitor. He was a comical figure, with old patched overalls and a sweater, several sizes too large, which hung from the bony shoulders as he shambled over toward Jim.

Lifting his battered old felt hat, the man greeted Jim in a surprisingly cultured tone. 'Good morning, young man. And what can I do for you?' The voice held resonance, with an orator's timbre, like the bass register of an organ. Immediately Jim was mesmerised by his presence. The scarecrow ambled forward, hand outstretched.

'I'm very pleased to make your acquaintance. My name is John Cartwright. Welcome to Shangri-La.' The hand that Jim took was warm with offered friendship, and had the grip of a younger man. It broke the spell.

'Ah'm sorry, sir. My name's Jim Whiteley. Ah was just lookin' at yer garden.'

Close up, the heavy-lidded eyes, slightly protuberant under tufted brows, were liquid brown, their depths gold-flecked, and they seemed to fill Jim's entire field of vision. They broke contact. John Cartwright was the first to speak.

'It's a pleasure to have a visitor. Would you like a cup of tea? The kettle is on.' Jim, still bemused, could only murmur, 'Thank you very much, I'd like that'.

The inside of the cabin was spartan but clean, and in the centre of the floor was a tortoise stove on which the kettle was singing. The lad stood awkwardly, hands at his sides, as John brewed the tea. He felt unsure of how to act in this strange situation. Cartwright turned and exclaimed,

'I'm so sorry, my friend, please take a seat.' The youth sank down gratefully on the stool beside the small deal table. His eye was caught by a painting on the wall, a landscape, which, to his uncultured eye, was wonderful. New to the art of conversation, he said, 'I like your paintin', Mester Cartwright.'

Jim found himself trying to emulate Cartwright's cultured tones. He went on, 'Did you paint it?'

'No, Jim, it's my wife's work, she did it just before she died.' Jim was contrite and his accent slipped. 'Ah'm sorry, sir, ah didn't know.'

John smiled. 'No, no, that's quite all right, it was all fifteen years ago.' He set two cups on the table. 'I'm sorry, it's goat's milk in the tea, it's all I have.'

'I didn't know you'd got a goat', said Jim as he sipped the tea. 'I didn't see one in your garden.'

'I keep her tethered among the trees. She once got into the garden and destroyed half my cabbages.' As they talked, Jim discovered that his host had been a schoolmaster and a lecturer. When his wife died from tuberculosis he had 'retired from the human race, to be left in peace with my memories'. Jim asked the obvious question.

'Don't you get lonely out 'ere, all on your own?'

'No, son, I have lots of friends.' He got up and went to a large chest at the end of the cabin. He opened it up and beckoned Jim to come over. The chest was full of books.

'Here they are, all of them', he said. 'Longfellow, Shakespeare, Dickens, Twain, all of them great writers. I can sail with Darwin, adventure with Kipling – as long as I have these, the world is my oyster.' He slapped himself on the cheek. 'I'm sorry Jim, I get carried away. It isn't often I have anyone to talk to. Do you read much?'

Jim was a little sheepish. 'To tell you the truth, Mister Cartwright, we don't 'ave many books in the 'ouse. We've got a Bible, an' a book called *The Scarlet Pimpernel*. I've read that four times.'

'Such a pity', the old man murmured as if to himself, compassion in his voice. 'Good minds going to waste'. He made a decision. 'Look, Jim, if I lend you a book, will you come back and tell me what you think of it?'

Jim replied gravely, 'I promise I will, Mister Cartwright, on my honour.' Cartwright chuckled at his serious expression, then sobered himself.

'Tell me, son, what do you mean by "on my honour"?'

Jim thought a little. 'Well, it means that if I don't do as I promised, ah'll let meself down, an' ah'll lose me reputation – people'd never trust me again.'

Cartwright nodded appreciatively and asked, 'What were you like at school, in English?'

'T'teacher used to say ah wrote t'best stories in t'class, but me writin' was rotten, so I got t'cane every time.'

'The blind fools, they're not fit to be called teachers', stormed John.

'The trouble I 'ad, I couldn't use what I'd learned. If I used big words everybody made fun of me.' The brown eyes were sympathetic.

'It was ever so, Jim, the prophet is without honour in his own country.' Seeing Jim's puzzled expression, he explained, 'The people close to you never appreciate your talents'. He bent over the chest of books murmuring, half to himself, 'I think we'll start you off with Kipling', and he handed the youth a large volume. It was bound in red morocco leather, with gold lettering on the spine which read *The Collected Works of Rudyard Kipling.* The edges of the leaves were gilded. Jim took it gingerly, as if it might break, and lapsed once again into his native tongue.

'Ah couldn't tek that Mester Cartwright, it's too . . . precious, ah wouldn't dare . . .' His voice faltered.

'I feel I can trust you Jim, but . . . please don't turn down the corners of the pages, it's a dirty habit.' The lad hugged the book to his chest.

'Thanks, Mister Cartwright, and thanks fer bein' . . . sympathetic?' He waited for approval for his choice of vocabulary, and John nodded. 'Can I come back next Wednesday?'

'Come any time you like, my friend, and you'll be welcome. I'll look forward to it. I'll have to go myself to attend my traps, I'm hoping to have rabbit stew for tea.' Waving to his new friend, Jim headed for Darnall, the book protected beneath his jacket.

*   *   *

Alice was busy with the tea when he came through the back door, clutching his chest with both arms. She registered alarm. 'What's wrong, Jimmy, 'ave yer got a pain?'

'Can't you call me Jim, Mam? Jimmy sounds like a babby's name.'

'All right, Jim. Now, come on, what's wrong wi' yer?' He took out the book and held it out to her. Her eyes widened in wonder.

'Wheer did yer get that? It's worth a lot o' money.'

'It's my new friend, Mester Cartwright, 'e lent it to me.' He told her all about his day, the words tumbling out. 'An' ah'm goin' again next Wednesday.' He glanced around the kitchen, suddenly aware. 'Wheer's me dad? 'E ought to be gettin' ready for work.'

'Ah've sent 'im ter t'doctor's wi' that chest, so 'e might be 'avin' one off terneet.' By way of an excuse, she added, ''E never 'as a day off. You remember that time when a stampin' fell on 'is foot. 'E could 'ardly walk, but 'e didn't 'ave an hour off. 'E ought ter look after 'issell better.'

Jim, sitting with the book, replied, 'Aye, ah've 'eard 'im cough before, but it weren't like it is now. It sounds as if 'e's tearin' summat.' He got up from the chair. 'Ah'm takin' this upstairs, Mam, 'cos ah've got ter feed t'pigs. Ah'll 'ave a read later on.'

Coming back downstairs, he heard his father's voice. 'Ah tell yer, ah'm awreight, Alice. Doctor Shaughnessy says ah've on'y got a bit o' bronchitis. It's an 'angover from t'winter, an' as'll be awreight when t'good weather comes.'

'Ne'er mind that, yer need t'ave one off.' Joe's face set in stubborn lines, but his chest heaved.

'Ah'm goin' ter work, Mother, an' that's me last word. Ah'm t'first 'and, an' if ah don't go, t'rest o' t'team'll 'ave ter go on flat hourly rate, an' they're not gerrin' as much as me in t'first place.' Alice knew when she was beaten, so she put his meal on the table.

'Awreight, Joe, you know best. Nah come an' get yer tea, love, or it'll be cold.' As Jim made his way to the back door, she added, 'An' *you* can get your *own* tea Jim, t'pigs can wait'.

Her tone implied that even if she couldn't handle the old one, she could make the young one toe the line.

★　　★　　★

After tea, Jim was given special dispensation to go in the parlour and read. As he settled down on the sofa, he heard Tom come in.

'Hallo, Mam.' There was a thump as a pair of boots were flung into the scullery. 'Wheer's ah Jim? Off wi' 'is pigs again?'

'No, 'e's in t'front room readin'.' As Tom made for the parlour door, her voice rose, 'An' leave 'im alone while 'e's quiet. Come an' get yer tea.' Silence returned.

Ensconced on the sofa, knees up, Jim was leafing through his wonderful book when 'Toomai of the Elephants' caught his eye. He began reading Kipling's immortal prose and the house on Kirby Road disappeared. Jim was immersed in the sight, sound and smell of India when the great Raj was in its heyday. Two hours later he was dragged away from the elephant's dance by his mother shaking him, saying, 'Jim, come on, it's bedtime. I've shouted yer three times, were yer asleep?'

He felt disoriented, pulled back through space and time. 'No, Mam, I was reading.' For a moment his Sheffield accent had vanished.

His mother continued, 'It must be good stuff yer reading.'

Jim was ecstatic. 'It's wonderful, Mam. Kipling must be t'best writer that ever lived.'

Alice ruffled the wiry brown thatch and sighed. 'Keep at it, son. I envy you, you've got it all to come. Just finish that story, then yer must go to bed.'

'All right, Mam.' Once more he was back in the jungle and the elephants stamped until the earth shook.

★   ★   ★

Each evening, when work was done, Jim re-entered the magical world between the red leather covers. Once more he was transported by the pen of the great author. The following Wednesday he was up and about by nine o'clock. As he was putting on his coat, he asked, a little hesitantly,

'Mam, could ah tek Mester Cartwright a loaf? 'E says it's the only thing 'e misses, bein' up there, an' ah'd like ter do summat for 'im.' Alice smiled.

'It's a good job ah baked yesterd'y. Pass me that newspaper.' She wrapped the loaf and put it in a brown paper bag. Handing it to him, she implored, 'An' try an' get 'ome in time fer tea'. He put the book in the carrier and replied,

'Thanks, Mam, you're lovely.' He kissed her on the cheek and dashed off. Alice stood holding the spot he had kissed, a small, secret smile curving her lips, though the lower one trembled.

Arriving at the forest retreat, Jim was welcomed warmly by the recluse. When he handed John the loaf, his thanks were effusive. 'Thank you, thank you, Jim. It's a very long time since I received a present.' He looked with admiration at the brown, crusty loaf. 'I'm going to enjoy that. I can't thank you enough.'

'It's 'ome-made. My mother made it.' He said this proudly. 'She's a good cook.'

'Well, please take my thanks to your good mother. Come in, Jim.' The lad sat down on the stool, the book in both hands.

'I want to thank you, Mister Cartwright. This book must be the best that was ever written.' John took the book and riffled the pages.

'I must say that you've kept it beautifully, Jim.' He thought a moment. 'How much have you read?'

'I've read five o' the stories, but ah liked 'Toomai' the best.' Cartwright sat down opposite.

'Rudyard Kipling is a fine author, but there are other authors, quite as good. It's up to you, my friend, but I'd like your opinion on an American author, Mark Twain. He wrote stories about a lad called Huckleberry Finn, who had lots of adventures with his negro friend. Would you like to try him and give old Kipling a rest?'

'Just as you like, Mister Cartwright. You know a lot more about it than I do.

51

I'd like to try all of 'em.' John gave a deep chuckle.

'All in good time! You see, no author is so good that he never wrote a bad book, yet most have at least one good book in them. It's best to try them all, in case you miss one.'

Jim, a little doubtful and afraid of ridicule, said, 'It's funny, I liked the smell of that book – the leather and the paper . . .' His voice trailed off, unsure.

John gave a slow smile. 'You're a man after my own heart. I've always loved the smell of books. All the wisdom of the ages is locked up in them, and the only key you need is curiosity. You have the key, Jim. Use it wisely and your horizons are boundless.' He smiled ruefully. 'I'm sorry, I didn't mean to preach, my lecturing days are over.'

Jim, still in the spell of the old man's vibrant baritone, said in a low voice, 'Please, go on, Mister Cartwright, I like to hear your voice.' John chuckled.

'Believe me, Jim, that voice was just a part of my stock-in-trade as a lecturer, just something I used to hold the attention of my audience. The voice was a lucky accident, the words you must learn. Also, you must feel strongly about your subject, and this will show itself as you speak.' He laughed again. 'You see, I'm lecturing again! Look, would you like some dinner. I'm afraid it's only rabbit stew and vegetables.' Jim was enthusiastic.

'Yes please, Mister Cartwright, I'd like it a lot.' They tucked into the food, and as they later sat back, replete, John asked, 'Do you want to come for a walk? I'm going to collect some herbs. I sell them to the herbalist's at Darnall.'

As they walked, John showed him the woodland in a new light, pointing out all the remedies that Mother Nature keeps in her cupboard, such as digitalis from the foxglove and belladonna from the deadly nightshade, with its purple and yellow flowers. He was shown comfrey for bruises, red clover for whooping cough and many more. Cartwright explained the inter-dependence of animals, plants and insects.

When they arrived back at the cabin, John's sack was full. The herbs were tied in bundles to dry, and they sat down and talked about religion, politics, work . . . in fact, life in general. Besides being a talented speaker, Cartwright was also a good listener, and he drew out of Jim all the desires, hopes and fears that young men are heir to.

The sun was low as Jim set off home with the collected works of Mark Twain in his carrier. His head was whirling with facts, ideas and feelings implanted by his mentor, seeds that would later blossom into real intellect.

Over the coming months, his mental capacity was to grow faster than his young, strong body. Yet he would be afraid to use this knowledge for fear of being set apart from his fellows. Among his own people, he would still use their language, knowing instinctively that he must hide his light behind a bushel.

* *

Chapter Seven

A FEW DAYS LATER, Jim drove Punch round to Ralph's place, helped by nudges from a stout stick. The pig weighed in at 319lbs. Ralph slapped Jim on the back.

'Yer've got a good un theer, lad. Yer ought ter get abaht . . . uh, fourteen quid at Armitage's.' Jim's mouth dropped open, he didn't realise that sort of money existed.

Ralph, seeing his disbelief, laughed and said, 'Look, Jim, you worked a year for that, yer've earned it.' He took the lifting strap from under Punch's ample belly and continued, 'While yer 'ere, yer might as well look at the sty ah were tellin' yer abaht. It'll need a good fettlin' aht, mind, as it's not been used fer a couple o' years.'

As they walked over to the sty, Jim asked, 'Who does it belong to? Is it anybody ah know?'

'It belonged to Missis Green's son, she lives on Dunkirk Square.'

'Ah know 'er, ah deliver 'er milk. She's a reight owd sourpuss.'

'Well don't pay 'er more than eighteen pence a week, that's all it's worth.' They stopped at the sty. 'There y'are Jim, it'll 'owd up ter twelve pigs, that.'

'Thanks, Ralph. When ah've selt Punch I'll go an' see 'er.'

Before setting off for Armitage's, he tied a piece of string to Punch's back leg as a restraint and, with the stick as a spur, he went up the lane to the main road. (It was indicative of Darnall at that time that no one thought it at all strange to see a pig being taken for a walk.) A few minutes later he was turning up Irving Street making for for the back yard of the shop. Knocking on the back door, he was rewarded by the appearance of the pimply-faced assistant who, in adenoidal tones, asked him what he wanted.

'Ah'd like ter see Mester Armitage, on business.'

'Awreight, wait 'ere, ah'll tell 'im.' The youth withdrew, the door closing. Two minutes later the pork butcher, a large, burly man in a blue-striped apron and straw boater, appeared.

'Good afternoon, Mester Armitage', said Jim in business-like tones, 'ah've come ter do you a favour. Ah've got a good three-'undred pounds o' prime pork 'ere, an' ah can mek you a good price.' Armitage, tight-lipped, bent down and examined Punch, then stood up, his face non-committal.

'Awreight, then, 'ow much d'yer want fer 'im?'

'Well, ter be fair, ah'll 'ave ter ask, uh . . . sixteen.' He was trembling inside. ''E's been fed on t'best y'know.'

The big man once more prodded the hams and shoulders of the luckless

Punch. 'No, lad, ah couldn't go 'igher than fourteen.'

Jim pretended to consider the offer. 'Tell yer what, Mester Armitage, bein' as ah know yer, ah'll let 'im go fer fifteen, but ah'm robbin' meself.' Armitage lit a fag as Jim leaned on the yard wall, prepared to wait. The butcher took a couple of draws of the fag, then gestured with his butcher's knife.

'Fourteen-pound ten ah'll gi'e yer, tek it or leave it.'

Jim hesitated before he said, 'Awreight, Mester Armitage, if yer'll throw in seven pork chops off 'im'.

'Done,' said Armitage, holding out his hand. 'Tie 'im up o'er theer,' indicating the shed, 'an' ah'll get yer money. Yer'll 'ave ter come in Tuesday fer t'chops.'

A few minutes later, Jim, astounded at his own business acumen, stood outside the shop and came to a decision. He walked up the road to the Bank, clutching the roll of notes, while a small inner voice whispered that this was blood money.

The manager was astounded that such a young lad wished not only to open an account but to deposit fourteen pounds – quite a tidy sum for those pre-inflation days. With his bank-book in his pocket, Jim made his way home to proudly inform his mother of his entry into the world of finance.

*   *   *

After demolishing a large plate of tripe and onions, our hero decided to go down to Dunkirk Square and negotiate for the pigsties. The door of the Green residence opened when he knocked, and the lady of the house, mousey hair pulled tightly back in a bun, asked, 'What do you want? Ah paid yer t'milk yesterd'y.'

Mrs Green's mouth, downcurved, with deep lines bracketing the thin lips, registered her disapproval of anything and everything. In her defence, it must be said that she had lost her husband, a roller in a steel mill, when a red-hot bar had come out of the rolls crooked, and took him where all good rollers go. Then, the army had taken her only son, leaving her permanently soured against the world. Jim knew nothing of this and dived in breezily.

'Afternoon, Mrs Green. Ah wonder if yer'd like ter rent me them pigsties o' yer son's? It'd be worth a bob a week ter yer.' Mrs Green sniffed, her crafty brain working overtime. She folded her arms under an ample bosom.

'Ah don't know as ah want ter rent 'em.'

'Well, it'd mek a nice bit o' money fer yer son ter come 'ome to, wun't it?'

She hesitated, but greed triumphed.

'Awreight then, but ah'll 'ave ter charge yer one an' tuppence.'

'Thanks Missis Green, 'ere's me first week's rent, an' could yer write me a receipt in 'ere?' He pulled out a dog-eared notebook and a stub of pencil. Surprised, the widow did as he asked, and the deal was closed.

The following day, after finishing his rounds, he took the cart round to the old hut, and with much struggling managed to get Judy and her brood into it. As he drove down the lane towards their new home, Ralph lifted his pipe in salute. He stopped and leaned over.

'Ah got it, Ralph, one-an'-tuppence a week. Oh aye, an' Armitage gen me fourteen-pound-ten fer t'boar an' threw in some pork chops as well.' Ralph chuckled.

'We'll mek a pigman o' thee yet, Jim.'

★   ★   ★

Alice was ironing when Jim returned and asked what there was for tea. His mother looked up as she bent to put the flat-iron back on the hob to heat up again, and replied, 'Ah'm gettin' some sausage an' we're 'avin' toad-in-the-'ole.'

Jim, deliberately casual, said, ''Ow do you fancy some pork chops?' Alice rubbed the iron on the rug to remove any soot, and answered, 'Don't be silly, it's Tuesday, an' yer know yer dad doesn't get paid while Friday.'

'Well ah'm goin' down to Armitage's to fetch some pork chops 'e owes me. Ah talked 'im into givin' me seven chops off Punch for part o' t'price.' She was overjoyed.

'Yer dad'll think it's 'is birthday. Ah'll do some baked potatoes an' Yorkshire puddin' wi' 'em, it'll buck 'im up a bit. 'E's not well at all, 'is chest dun't get any better. Ah made 'im some linseed, liquorice an' lemon but it 'asn't touched it.'

'It's all that smoke 'e works in, it clogs 'is lungs', said Jim. 'Mister Cartwright told me all about it. 'Is wife died because their 'ouse was close to a meltin' furnace an' t'fumes got into it. She died o' tuberculosis, an' that's why 'e lives in t'wood, where there's fresh air.' The young forehead creased. 'Ah wish me dad could get outa that place.'

Alice was about to reply, but mimed a 'ssh' as she heard Joe coming downstairs. She continued, 'Right then, Jim, you get off to Armitage's.'

As Joe reached up to the mantelpiece for his Woodbines, she said, ''Ow about that Joe? Pork chops on a Tuesday! Jim's got 'em for us, they're off 'is pig.'

Joe sat down with his paper and replied, grinning, 'Th'art a good un, lad, it's a pity tha can't kill one every week.' He put on his spectacles, now held with a piece of elastic on one side. Jim watched him, noting the fast breathing and the stubbled cheeks, fast becoming hollow. His heart sank with a nameless dread. Walking out into the yard he heard his father's tearing cough as he struggled to clear his lungs of accumulated filth from the furnaces.

When he got to Armitage's, the butcher greeted him with open arms. 'Hello, Jim, I'm glad yer came in, ah've got yer chops ready.' He put one parcel on the counter followed by another. 'That pig were better than I expected so ah've thrown in some liver. If yer've got any more, ah'll 'ave 'em off yer.' The lad flushed with pleasure.

'Thanks, Mister Armitage, ah might 'ave a sow in a few weeks, ah've not made me mind up yet.'

'Well, don't forget me if yer decide.' He turned to the customers. 'Yes, Missus, what can ah do for you?'

Jim went home triumphant, carrying his precious burden. Coming through the scullery he heard his mother's voice.

'If yer won't do it fer yerself will yer do it fer me? Yer losin' weight, an' if yer don't do summat about it yer'll go into 'ospital on your back.' Jim could not contain himself.

'Mam's reight, Dad. Next thing you know you'll 'ave tuberculosis.' His tongue stumbled over the unfamiliar syllables, but he went on bravely. 'If your lungs get wasted, they can't put 'em back, so why don't yer go an' see somebody?'

Joe's face suffused with blood. 'Ah don't need a snotty-nosed kid like you ter tell me my business, wi' yer big words. Ah suppose yer've been talkin' ter Mister bloody high-and-mighty Cartwright.' He broke off, panting. Jim stood up to him.

'Yes, I 'ave, Dad, an' 'e's a very intelligent bloke. 'E says you ought ter . . .' He broke off as his father roared, 'Shut up!' and delivered a full-blooded backhander to the lad's face. Tears sprang to Jim's eyes, but inherited stubbornness prevented him from touching the injured cheek. He turned on his heel and went into the scullery, to stand gazing stonily out of the window, but not seeing.

The normally submissive Alice glared at her husband, her face a mask of fury. Before she had time to speak, the now-deflated Joe forestalled her. In a tired voice he murmured,

'Awreight, Alice, ah know.' His chest inside the old union shirt pumped like a bellows as he walked to the scullery. He turned the unresisting Jim by one shoulder and placed a hand on the other, noticing with some surprise that their faces were almost level. His son, the red welt standing out on his cheek, refused to raise his eyes. His father spoke in a strained, unnatural tone.

'Please, Jim, there were no excuse fer what ah did. Yer were reight, but ah know 'ow bad me chest is, an' . . . ah'm scared, son. I 'ad to hit out at summat, an' you 'appened ter get in t'way. Will yer forgive me?'

''Course, Dad . . . and look, if it's money that's worryin' you, ah've got twenty-three pound odd in t'bank an' you can 'ave t'lot.'

His father grinned sheepishly. 'No, son, ah can't tek that. Ah'm in t'sick an' divide club at work, so we'll be awreight fer a few weeks.' As they went back into the kitchen Joe continued, 'Yer've made me see sense, ah'll do as t'quack tells me, an' see if ah can get missen reight.'

Alice had her back to them as she wiped away the tears. She turned and said to them, with forced cheerfulness,

'Ah think we ought ter go out for a drink tonight, Joe, ah'm fed up o' bein' stuck in t'house all week.'

'Good idea lass, an' we'll tek Jim. If we go down Attercliffe, 'e'll pass for eighteen, an' 'e's workin' as 'ard as most men. Fancy a pint, son?'

'Aye, ah do, it's took yer long enough ter ask me. Ah'll get changed.' He headed upstairs, leaving Joe and Alice in each others' arms.

*   *   *

Within a month Joe was in Lodge Moor Hospital. For three weeks he was treated by the specialists and got used to sleeping with the window open. George Bolsover allowed Jim to take his mother up there in the cart twice a week, and by the end of Joe's stay the sweet air sweeping in from the moorlands of Moscar Top had worked wonders.

When he was discharged, the doctor insisted on two weeks convalescence at Skegness. Although she hated losing him, Alice put on a brave face, and it was not until the train pulled out of Darnall Station that she let go. Jim, now the man of the house, comforted her as they walked down Station Road and back to the house, which now seemed empty.

Jim sat staring into the fire as his mother mashed the tea. Breaking the silence, he remarked, in gravelly tones similar to his father's, 'Ah don't know 'ow ah'm goin' ter do it, Mam, but some'ow ah'm gonna do summat about this smoke that's killing people.'

His voice had acquired some of Cartwright's charisma. His mother listened spellbound, this was a Jim that she had never encountered. He continued, 'In t'Bible – John read it me – it says that man's years upon the earth are three-score years and ten, an' yet men – an' women – are dyin' just so that some gaffer that they might never see can live to be seventy up Fulwood, while people down 'ere are dyin' at fifty with TB.'

He told her about his visit to Hyde Park and finished, 'An' that smoke even *looked* poisonous, yet people are breathing that muck.' His mother shook herself, breaking the spell, and murmured slowly, in wonder at her son's eloquence, 'Do you know, Jim, you've got me believin' you. Ah think you might even do it, but in God's name, ah don't know 'ow.'

Then she continued, as if to herself, 'John Cartwright must be a wonderful man'. Mentally, she compared Jim with his brother. These days Tom never seemed to be in, he was either up at the 'tossing ring' in High Hazels Park or out boozing. Still, she recalled that Joe was the same until he was about thirty, so she couldn't blame him too much.

A few days later the postman delivered a card and a letter. The card was a comic one – to be propped on the sideboard – but the letter Alice kept, to read secretly. In it Joe said many things he had never said in thirty years of marriage. As she sat reading it for the third time, Jim came in from work, and she looked up, eyes liquid.

'What's up, Mam? Is summat wrong?' She folded the letter and replaced it in the envelope.

'No, Jim, nowt's wrong. Everything couldn't be better.' The lad went to the sink to get washed, puzzling on the enigma of women.

★   ★   ★

The two weeks passed slowly, but eventually Alice and Jim stood together on the platform at Darnall Station, both in their best. The others, Sally and Tom, were both working, but mother and son gazed anxiously as the train came to a halt. A door opened further up the platform and a stocky figure wearing blue serge and sporting his bowler hat at a rakish angle stepped out carrying the old cardboard suitcase. He dropped the case as Alice came flying up the platform, almost losing her hat in the process. Jim followed, a little more sedately.

After embracing her long-lost husband, she stepped back and held his arms, inspecting him. The sunken cheeks had filled and there was a flush of health in them for the first time in months.

'By, Alice', Joe confided, 'that's t'longest fortneet ah've ever spent'. Stroking his moustache, he added, 'Look, ah've even trimmed me 'tache'.

'Aye, Joe, it looks good, but ah'll 'ave ter get that shirt in t'wash, it's scruffy.' Jim stepped forward and Joe shook his hand, a little self-consciously, saying,

'Tha gets bigger every time ah see thee. Tha'll soon be bigger than me.' He tugged at his starched collar. 'Let's gerrome and get this bloody thing off.' Jim picked up the suitcase and they went down the platform, Joe with an arm round each of them.

That night Jim insisted on taking his family to the *Dog and Partridge* for a drink. During the evening, Tom offered his father a Woodbine, but Jim shook his head.

'No son, ah gi'en 'em up. T'doctors said ah were gerrin' enough smoke dahn at Brown Bayley's for nowt, wi'out payin' fer it. I 'an't 'ad a fag fer five weeks, so ah think ah can manage wi'out 'em.'

There was the lonely, dying sound of a train whistle as two people lay later that evening in the old brass bedstead. Joe whispered some of the things that he'd said in his wife's treasured letter, and Alice was whole again.

58

❋ ❋

JIM'S VISITS to the cabin in the woods continued and his horizons broadened with each precious book that John loaned him. One grey Wednesday, when the red leaves fell signalling autumn's onset, he traced the now-familiar path through the woods. The squirrels chattered, discussing the serious business of winter storage.

A short way from the cabin, as he trudged immersed in his thoughts, Jim was pulled out of his reveries by a voice hailing him through the trees. It was John, and after a brief hello, they walked on in a companionable silence which Jim was the first to break.

'It's strange, John, but ev'ry autumn ah start to feel a bit . . . sad when t'leaves start to fall.'

'Yes, I get something of the same. I think that at twilight and at autumn we all have a small dying, a taste of what the real thing will be. Yet, for myself, the more twilights that I endure the easier it is to contemplate that last long winter with no spring to follow.' Jim selected a stem of grass to chew and replied 'Oh, you've got a lot more springs yet, John'.

There was a pause before the old man replied in a reflective tone. 'I'm seventy-four, that's four years over my allotted span, so every year now is a bonus. I've even become curious about what comes after.'

'Tell me, John, what do *you* think comes after?' Cartwright stopped and the lad was fixed by the gold-flecked eyes. The deep baritone voice rumbled.

'Since the birth of time men have asked that question, and many better men than I have stepped through the door. As far as we know, none have come back to tell us of it except through spiritualists or mediums, who I distrust. Arthur Conan Doyle, a great author, believed implicitly in the afterlife, and he even named the date and time of his return, but he never came.' They walked on, and he continued, 'For an old man such as myself, re-incarnation seems a rather attractive possibility. I find the idea of experiencing life again through a new young body quite irresistible. Unfortunately, I shall not know until the day arrives.'

By this time they had reached the cabin. The kettle was put on and Jim stoked up the dying fire. As he straightened up he said, 'Thanks for t'book, John, it was very good, but ah found t'white whale a bit . . . unbelievable. Ah thought 'e used a lot more words than 'e needed. What 'ave you got for me this week?'

Cartwright smiled as he spooned tea into the pot. 'How do you feel about trying some poetry?'

'Ah don't know. Isn't poetry a bit . . . snobbish?' The old man chuckled. 'Try it, Jim. You like singing, don't you?' Jim nodded. 'Songs are merely poetry set to music. I'll lend you some Longfellow. His most famous work is *Hiawatha*, but you may find it very different from the poetry that you know. The rhythm is supposed to suggest the chanting of a Red Indian tribe – read it out loud if you find yourself alone, it's quite magnificent. Allow yourself to feel the rhythm of the words. Let Longfellow speak to you. I won't tell you any more in case I spoil a great experience.'

'Awright, John, ah'll try it, but ah think ah might be too stupid for that stuff.'

'Don't underestimate yourself, Jim. When I was your age I had to fight for an education. You have a good brain, and I'm only guiding you the best I know how. The rest is up to you.'

'Ah couldn't be a lecturer like you, I 'aven't got the knowledge or the way you put words together.'

'Ah, Jim, education can open the door to many things, not only lecturing. Many you will find involve the art of public speaking, however; parliament, the stage, the ministry. In each of these professions your purpose is to transmit a message, to persuade others to accept your beliefs, to impose your will on them. Soon your voice will be fully formed, and if you practice you can make it fill a hall. All you need is a little guidance and a great deal of confidence.'

The kettle boiled and John brewed the tea. They sat down to have their usual chat about anything that came into their minds, and John listened soberly to Jim's opinions. Joe's illness entered the conversation, and Jim repeated the speech he had made to his mother about Sheffield's deadly blanket of smoke. This time, uninhibited, he spoke at more length.

The old man listened, admiration dawning as he heard his pupil marshalling his facts and speaking with real feeling. Cartwright was silent for some seconds after Jim had finished, then a smile creased the weather-beaten face and he said, 'I thought you said you couldn't be a lecturer. You've just given *me* a lecture, and it was thoroughly convincing. And you're only sixteen, my boy. Imagine what the future might hold!'

Jim grinned, unsure. 'I didn't know I was doing it, John, it just came out.'

'That's how it should be. If it comes from the heart, it is genuine. Passion and conviction are the keys to an audience's attention.' He slapped Jim on the back. 'Today you have made an old man happy. I thought my teaching days were over, but you've turned out to be one of the best pupils I have ever had. I only hope that I'm around when you reach your peak.'

★   ★   ★

Once again, it was late when Jim set off for home, carrying his latest book. Passing the terminus, he glanced up Main Road. Outside Hedge's he saw Sally talking to someone he didn't recognize, a tall, good-looking man wearing a trilby hat. He stored the knowledge for future information and went on his way.

When Sally came in half-an-hour later she was in a big rush. 'Ah've got to be ready in an hour, ah'm goin' out.' Jim, who was sitting with his book, said slyly, 'Wouldn't be owt to wi' that ugly-lookin' bloke you were talkin' to on t'terminus, would it?' He took cover as Sally attacked him.

"'E's better lookin' than you, you look like one o' yer pigs – pig-face!' She said to Alice, 'Honest Mam, 'e's a nice bloke. 'E's a foreman at Cammell's an' 'e's takin' me to t'*Lyceum*. Ther's a play on 'e wants to see. We're goin' to t'Bodega café first for tea, an' ah'm meetin' 'im at 'arf past seven.' She dashed upstairs.

At twenty-past-seven, as Sally was about to go out, Alice said, 'Let's 'ope this one doesn't get a cigar in *'is* face.' Sally turned, furious.

'Ah'll kill that Joan when ah see 'er. She'd no right to tell yer.'

Alice laughed. 'I 'eard it from Mrs Manterfield at t'chipshop, she were four seats away from yer that neet. Most o' Darnall knew about it, that's t'reason 'is dad chucked 'im out. It worked out fer t'best as far as your reputation's concerned.' Sally felt mollified and dashed off to keep her date.

★   ★   ★

Jim had just fed his pigs and stood for a minute looking at Judy before setting off for Ralph's. He leaned on the wall as Ralph was mucking out the sty and asked, 'What do *you* think, Ralph. Should ah sell Judy or keep 'er for breedin'?' The pigman straightened up and leaned on his shovel. He spat on the floor, then replied. 'Well, Jim, if yer put 'er to pig again now, t'others'll be nowheer near ready for sale when she pigs. Ah think ah'd sell 'er an' save one o' t'new uns fer breedin'. In any case, when t'little uns get a bit bigger yer not gonna get enough swill fer 'em, so t'money from t'sow'll 'elp ter buy feed.'

Jim nodded. 'That's just about what I thought. Thanks Ralph.'

'Awreight, lad, but don't let 'er go fer fourteen-an'-'arf, there must be another forty pound on 'er, an' she 'an't made *too* much fat.' He went back to work with his shovel.

Three days later, Jim was to be seen again taking a pig for its last walk, but this time his account at the bank was swelled by sixteen pounds. As he left the bank, the book in his pocket read *'thirty pounds, two shillings and sevenpence'*. His wages, even now, were only twelve-and-six and he was constantly told by his mates in the steel works to come and get some real money. But his stock reply was, 'It's worth a pound a week to stay out o' them places. Ah'd sooner stop out 'ere where ah can breathe.'

★   ★   ★

As Jim went on his rounds on the morning of November 11th, 1918, there was suppressed excitement wherever he went. In the morning papers the headlines shouted CESSATION OF HOSTILITIES and went on to say that there was to be a cease-fire at 11.00 am that morning. When eleven o'clock came, Jim was going up Irving Street and all hell broke loose. All at the same time all the bells of every church in Sheffield were rung, and all the factory hooters blown in celebration of the event that had been so long awaited.

As he came back down the main road Jim drew near the 'Iron Duke' , and there, in front of the urinal with his portable pulpit, was Mr Smith, the blind evangelist. The tall, gaunt figure was a regular visitor to Darnall. From his commanding position, backed by the green-painted monument, he would exhort the habitués of the *Bradley, Wellington* and *Duke of York* to 'come to the Lord and forsake the demon drink'.

A favourite trick of the Darnall urchins was to creep up behind him and throw sand on his braille Bible. This drove him to refer to them in anything but biblical terms, which made it all the more fun.

On this day of all days, this instrument of the Lord's work was having a field-day. The theme of his sermon was, 'And the power of the Lord Almighty has shattered the swords of the ungodly and they shall be cast into the uttermost reaches of Hell, yea, into fire and brimstone shall they be cast to suffer the everlasting tortures of the damned'. And, in a lower tone, 'And if you little sods don't bugger off, ah'll kill yer!'

The days wore on. The only places that saw any change were the churches and pubs as ordinary people celebrated the end of four years of uncertainty, many with sons and daughters still on the battlefield. Everyone knew that it would be weeks, maybe months, before their loved ones returned, and this thought tempered their celebrations. There was no flag-waving, no brass bands, only thankfulness that it was finally over and the country could return to normal.

When Jim got home, his mother was gazing wistfully at a photograph of Sam, looking handsome in his uniform. She shook her head and said, 'It's too bad, Jim, here's one casualty of war who won't be comin' 'ome.' She quietly hid the photograph behind the sideboard on which it had once stood proudly.

★   ★   ★

During the following months, the young men trickled back, many of them in good health, but many, too, who would never recover. Many of their injuries were serious, but the most distressing to see were the cases of gas-poisoning or shell-shock. Young men had breathed in the chlorine, mustard gas or Lewisite or had suffered terrible disfigurement where the liquid gas had ravaged their exposed flesh.

More insidious, and less obvious, was the effect of shell-shock on minds that had been unable to withstand the terrible concussion brought on by near-misses, or the self-inflicted thunder of our own gun barrages. These luckless victims could be seen in the streets, trembling, seemingly afraid of their own shadows.

Jim, after seeing some of these human parodies, asked John, 'What's 'appened to them John? 'Ow can one man do this to another?'

Cartwright thought a moment, then replied, 'How can I explain? If someone were to hit you hard enough and often enough, eventually you would climb into a hole and refuse to come out, wouldn't you?' Jim nodded. 'When the brain has suffered repeated concussion, it will finally climb into a cave within itself, and when that has happened, it will cease to function correctly. As to your second question, I can't give you an answer. All I can say is that if you take a man with no morals and put him in a position of power, be it with a rifle or a pen, eventually he will abuse that position.'

Jim persisted. 'Yes, but why does an *ordinary* bloke go to war? An ordinary man who's kind to kids an' animals? 'Ow do they get *them* to kill people? I'm not just talkin' about us. I don't think t'French an' t'Germans want to kill each other, either. Millions of people 'ave died since 1914. Why?'

Cartwright gave a wry smile. 'You're asking questions to which you didn't really expect an answer. You put over your argument very well.'

'I just wanted to put into words what I've been thinkin'. I'm tryin' to make some sense of what I see happenin'.'

As usual, the discussion continued, but this time they spoke together as equals rather than as teacher and pupil.

★   ★   ★

Sally's young man, Richard Appleby, was a softly-spoken man, two years her senior, and he proved to be a steadying influence on the headstrong Sally. When she first brought him home, her father seemed to mistrust him, maybe because he was a foreman and therefore a symbol of authority. However, as they talked, Joe found that they had interests in common, such as Sheffield Wednesday, and after that first visit they were on first-name terms.

The couple were allowed use of the parlour for their courting, and it was evident to everyone that they were hopelessly in love. Richard would buy little presents for his girl, and at times he even bought treats for Alice or Joe.

One supper-time, Sally had been out with her young man and came in flushed and happy, waving her left hand at her mother and father. On the third finger was a diamond ring. She explained rapturously, 'Richard's asked me to marry 'im an' 'e's given me this ring. It was 'is mother's, an' I think it's beautiful.'

Then to her father she said, 'Dad, 'e wants to come an' ask you about us gettin' married'. Joe studied her over his glasses and smiled. 'By the look o' thee, lass, it won't mek a bit o' bloody difference what ah say. Any road, yer twenty-two, an' yer can marry anybody yer like. But if it meks yer feel any better, ah don't think yer'll find a better bloke. 'E's reight fer thee.' Sally came over and kissed her father on his developing bald patch, and he grunted as he returned to studying form.

★   ★   ★

It was two weeks to Christmas and the house was empty except for Jim who, as usual, was reading. The book this time was H.G. Wells' *The Time Machine* and he was deep into it when Tom came in, threw his boots into the scullery and sat down in the other easy chair. Jim got the feeling that he wanted to talk so he marked his place and put down the book.

'You're 'ome early, Tom, what's the matter, run outa coal?'

His brother remained silent for a few moments then said, 'Owd Len Goodwin's packin' in t'coal business an' nob'dy in t'yard wants any men.'

Jim shrugged. 'Well, ah reckon they're wantin' men down at Spear and Jackson's, an' it's not a bad firm to work for.'

Tom slumped deeper in the chair and sighed. 'Ah don't want ter go in t'firms, ah want ter *see* places. Ah'm fed up o' t'carry-on round 'ere.'

'It's no good you goin' ter t'Army, they're chuckin' 'em out by t'undred.

64

T'same wi' t'Navy.' Tom turned to look at his brother, his face animated.

'Ah were talkin' to a bloke in t'*Wellington*. 'E can get me in wi' a firm that does construction work, y'know, they put up girder-work all o'er t'country. It's good money, but ah'd be workin' in Manchester fer a start.'

'If it dun't work out you can allus come 'ome. T'on'y trouble is, me mam isn't goin' ter like it. If I were you, I'd 'ave a word wi' me dad first, an' 'e'll break it to her.'

When Tom finally broached the subject to Joe, the reply surprised him. 'Ah wain't pretend ah like yer goin', son, but if ah interfere, instead o' goin' 'appy, yer'll go wi' a chip on yer shoulder. Any road, ah've nowt ter brag abaht. what ah've done wi' me life, so p'raps yer'll find summat better. Ah say, good luck ter thee.'

Ten days later Tom was packed and ready to catch the seven o'clock from Victoria Station. Before he went for his tram, his father had a last exhortation for him.

'So long Tom, and fer Christ's sake watch thissen when yer up theer, it's a bloody long way dahn. Don't ferget ter write an' let us know 'ow yer goin' on.' Alice could only manage a husky 'Goodbye Tom, look after yourself'. She kissed him and held him for long seconds, then he was away, through the back door, with the old cardboard suitcase.

★   ★   ★

The days passed quickly, and on Christmas Day the whole family was together for dinner. Tom, now working in South Shields, had managed to get home for a few days, and Joan arrived, proudly displaying evidence of Joe's first grandchild, while a grinning Bob was congratulated on proving himself.

Latecomers were Sally and Richard who announced that they were getting married in March. The happy events seemed to offset the fact that Sam had not been heard of since that fateful night two years before, and no-one mentioned his name. Still, Alice said a secret prayer for her first-born, wherever he might be.

Chapter Nine

THE HOLIDAY went ahead with the usual ingestion of copious amounts of best bitter, but on the day after Boxing Day they had to return to work, back to the humdrum round that was a working family's life.

In late February, when the last of the snow was dirty in the streets, the house was once more in turmoil, this time for Sally's wedding. Alice and Sally worked on the trousseau and Jim got permission to use the beautiful gig again.

As with Joan's wedding, it was a perfect occasion. The gig could have been Cinderella's coach and Sally a princess as they swept up to the church door. After the ceremony, as Jim followed one of the bridesmaids upstairs to the reception at the *Duke of York*, the nicely-rounded bottom in front of his eyes was too much to resist. He reached forward and, none too gently, pinched it.

The response was immediate. The girl turned and hit him with the first thing that came to hand, her posy. Repeated blows reduced the bouquet to shreds, and all Jim could do was to stand and laugh, which only increased the fury of his assailant. He took most of the blows on his forearm, which was raised defensively, then managed to choke out, 'Look, I'm sorry, I'm *sorry*, I'll be'ave meself.'

The girl stood there, above him, flushed with her exertions and looked down at the ruined posy. Suddenly she was giggling. Pointing at him with the wreckage of the posy she warned him, between giggles, 'Don't *ever* do that again, whatever your name is'.

Jim held out his hand and, to his amazement, she took it. 'I'm Jim Whiteley, I'm Sally's dim brother. I go around annoying girls.'

She grinned, and replied in a husky contralto, 'My name's Mary Wilson, I'm a friend of Sally's, and I bash boys who do what you did.' The giggling started again as they carried on up the stairs.

Sitting down to the boiled ham tea, Jim found himself opposite Mary, and they smiled at each other across the table. He saw an attractive oval face, framed with blonde hair, softly waved, with laughing blue eyes under arching brows. He noted the slightly snub nose, and his gaze came to rest on the generous, full-lipped mouth, now parted in a smile, revealing teeth like a row of pearls. What he *didn't* realise as he began to lay plans, was that Mary was the little minx whose bottom he had pinched when he was six years old in Sunday school. If he had known, he would have undoubtedly have congratulated himself on his good taste.

When the trestle tables had been cleared away and the guests were gathered round the small tables with drinks, Jim, who was sitting with his parents, searched the room for the engaging Miss Wilson. He was so engrossed that he had not heard his mother. 'Jim, I've spoken to you twice, an' yer've ignored me.'

'I'm sorry, Mam, I was just lookin' for somebody.'

Alice chuckled and murmured to Joe, 'Ah bet that somebody's got blond 'air an' blue eyes.'

Jim had the good grace to blush, but at that moment caught sight of Mary, sipping orange juice with the other bridesmaid at the far end of the room. Her slightly urchin face screwed into a menacing expression and she made a small fist, but the pretence fell as her expression yielded to a laugh that she couldn't contain.

Joe remarked, eyes crinkling. 'Ah don't think 'e's with us, Alice'. Jim turned round, startled. 'Ah just asked yer if yer wanted another 'arf.'

Jim grinned. 'Yes, thanks, ah would. The time was approaching eight and Richard persuaded his brother Stan to take a turn on the piano. He was busking his way through *Daisy, Daisy* when Jim, taking his courage in both hands, went across to Mary, weaving his way between the dancers.

'Would you like to dance, Mary?' He was out of his depth with girls, but this was one that he didn't want to lose. Mary smiled apologetically, 'I'm not very good at it, I'm afraid.'

'Don't let that worry you. I've got two left feet so we can learn together.' After a little persuasion, the girl allowed herself to be led onto the floor, and from the moment he placed his hand on her slight, young waist Jim was in seventh heaven for the rest of the evening. He discovered that she lived up on Oliver's Mount, Darnall's equivalent of San Francisco's 'Nob Hill', and that her father managed a hide and skin business near the Shambles in town. She helped her dad with the accounts, she liked reading, and she used to go to Darnall Church School. Making conversation, Jim asked, 'Did you go to Sunday School there?'

'Yes, I went every week.' She chuckled. 'And I went to the Band of Hope. I was a good little girl.'

'Oh, I only went there once an' I was chucked out. My mother says . . .' He paused as a glimmer of light began to form. 'Will you excuse me a minute?' He went over to where his mother was sitting.

'Mam', he asked, 'you know when I went to Sunday School, didn't you say I got thrown out for nippin' a lass's bum?'

Alice smiled. 'Aye, yer did. 'Er father sent us a note sayin' that our 'ooligan son 'ad attacked 'is daughter. Why?'

'Were 'er name Mary Wilson?' His mother's forehead crinkled in thought.

'Ah think it was, she lived up on Oliver's Mount.' Jim chuckled.

'Thanks Mam.' He made his way back to Mary's table and sat down.

'Mary, when you went to Darnall Church, do you remember a lad nippin' your bottom?'

'It's funny you should say that. I was talking to old Mrs Penrose at last Watchnight Service, we were laughing about that. My dad went mad.'

Jim gave a sly grin. 'Do you know the lad that did it?'

Mary looked puzzled and asked, 'No I don't know who . . .' and then light dawned and she started giggling. 'Was it you?'

As Jim nodded, they both collapsed into helpless laughter. Later, but much too soon for Jim, Mary announced, that she had to leave.

'I'm sorry, Jim, but I promised I'd be home for ten o'clock.' She started putting on her coat and her gallant companion jumped up and helped her into it, asking nervously, 'Would you mind if I walked you 'ome?'

'No, I wouldn't. It'll be nice having a strong man to protect me.' Jim's chest swelled as he said goodnight to the family.

It was a beautiful starlit night, and as they walked hand-in-hand, Jim pointed out the constellations as he had learned them from John Cartwright. All the time he was acutely conscious of the lovely girl at his side. For her part, Mary was blessing the impulse that had made this rugged young man assault her person in such a cavalier manner. Still hand-in-hand, they stood in the moonlight outside the house on Oliver's Mount. Jim asked hopefully, 'Can I see you again? We could go to see a show or somethin'. Will you be free next Sat'day night?'

Mary pretended to consider. 'Yes, that would be nice, Jim, thank you.' The lad could have whooped with joy, but restrained himself.

'Right Mary, I'll call for you at seven.' He didn't let go of her hand, desperate to prolong the contact. She made as if to go, then turned to him and in that husky voice breathed, 'Goodnight, Jim.'

Raising herself on tiptoe, she kissed him on the lips then ran up the path. Her adoring man was left with her sweet breath in his nostrils and the memory of petal-soft lips on his.

An ecstatic Jim floated down Handsworth Hill with his head in the clouds. Suddenly he howled like a banshee and ran headlong until he was brought back to earth by bumping into his mother and father. They were crossing from the terminus, so he walked on with them. His father looked him up and down and remarked, 'Tha'rt looking chuffed wi' thissen!'

Jim answered, obliquely, 'What did you think to Mary?'

Alice smiled knowingly. 'She seemed a nice lass, what we saw of 'er. You two got on like a 'ouse afire.'

Jim didn't hide his enthusiasm. 'She's wonderful. I'm takin' 'er out next Sat'day.' His mother and father exchanged glances, then nodded. Their boy was growing up.

★   ★   ★

68

On his next day off, Jim made his usual trek through the forest. This time, when he saw John, he was shocked, for the weather-beaten face, without it's usual flush of health, looked jaundiced. For the first time he realised how old his friend was. Until now, the vitality and sheer presence of the man had disguised his age, but now the weight of seventy-five years was showing in the bowed frame and trembling hand. John spoke, his voice still vibrant.

'Good morning, Jim, I haven't seen you for a week or two. I hope you haven't been ill.' Jim felt a pang of conscience, because it had been three weeks since he last came.

'I'm sorry I 'aven't been to see you, but I 'ave been very busy, and it was our Sally's wedding on Sat'day.' He felt in his pocket. 'I've brought you a piece of wedding cake.' He handed over the serviette-wrapped packet.

'Thank her for me and, please, wish her much happiness.' He sank down in his chair as Jim filled the kettle and stoked the stove.

'You're not lookin' at all well, John, you'll 'ave to look after yourself.' Cartwright gave a tired grin.

'Don't worry, Jim. A long time ago, a doctor told me that I wouldn't live two years. The last attack was ten years ago. The doctors call it mitral stenosis, the valves don't work properly. I have the medicine and I'm picking up nicely, so don't distress yourself.'

The kettle was singing and Jim brewed the tea. He brought John up-to-date with his news. 'When I was at the wedding I met a girl and we got talking. I'm taking her out on Sat'day, but I don't know where to take her.'

The old man smiled. 'I'm delighted. I was wondering how long it would be before you discovered the opposite sex. As regards where to take her, don't you think it would be nice to ask her where *she* would like to go?'

Jim looked sheepish. 'Why didn't I think of that?' They finished the tea and, as Jim stood up, Cartwright asked, almost anxiously, 'Surely you're not going, Jim? I was looking forward to a chat.'

'Not just yet. First of all I'm going to stock you up with everything you need.' He went out of the door saying, 'Won't be long'. John read for a while then the book dropped and he dozed. An hour-and-a-half later the water churn had been filled, the goat had been tethered close to the cabin and there was a huge pile of wood ready for use. Hanging in the rafters were a rabbit and two pigeons, the fruit of Jim's foray round the traplines.

'There y'are, John, that'll save you goin' out for a couple o' days, then I'll be up to see you again. Is there anything else you might need?'

'No, thank you, Jim, you've done it all.' He reached down into the old chest and took out some papers. He leafed through them, unfolded one and passed it over the table. 'Read that, Jim', he said.

The document began: *'I, John Cartwright, being of sound mind, do bequeath all of my worldly goods to James Henry Whiteley of thirty-two Kirby Road in the parish of Darnall'* and went on to detail the few possessions. Jim read it soberly, then refolded it.

'John, you can't do this, you must have relations somewhere, somebody you can leave everything to.'

John shook his head sadly. 'I have no- one. I had a daughter, once. She married a lawyer. I haven't seen her for ten years. She didn't want to know an old tramp. There won't be much, but if you take the back off my wife's picture you will find fifty pounds. It will be enough to take care of any funeral expenses. I hope you will do this for me.'

Jim was aghast. 'I wouldn't know what to do.'

'Don't worry, I shall arrange everything.' He handed the lad a business card. 'Just go to this solicitor in Paradise Square and he will give you all the assistance you require.'

'Well, thanks for trustin' me, but I 'ope it'll be a long time before I need to do it.'

John smiled. 'So do I, but I should like to think that I shall have at least one mourner at my funeral.' When he saw Jim's woebegone expression, he added, 'But it could be years before it happens.'

By the time Jim left, Cartwright was looking much improved and the tone of the conversation had become more optimistic.

★   ★   ★

On the following Saturday afternoon, after his milk round, Jim filled the tin bath, and with the aid of carbolic soap and a scrubbing brush he gave himself the best bath he'd had since his mother last did it. Looking a little like a boiled lobster, he donned his white shirt and blue serge trousers which had been left to press under his mattress and, with difficulty, put in studs and cuff links.

In honour of the occasion he had been to Springs' outfitters and, for the princely sum of elevenpence had bought himself one of the new turn-down collars and a new tie. He had been assured by the shopwalker that all the gentlemen were wearing them now. With his new finery and a new white handkerchief in his top pocket, Jim set off to meet his inamorata.

He was a quarter-of-an-hour early and waited impatiently outside Cheetham's grocers, where he would be able to see Mary approaching. It was six-fifty-five by Darnall Church clock when he spied, in the distance, a trim figure coming towards him. Neat ankles showed below the long skirt, and on her blonde hair was a broad-brimmed straw hat, trimmed with a pale blue ribbon.

As the vision came nearer, Jim ran a hand over his unruly brown thatch and straightened the handkerchief in his breast pocket. He walked to meet her, heart pounding. He took her little hand in his and his heart was in his eyes as he said, 'Mary, you look beautiful.'

The girl looked up at him from under long lashes and her voice was light as she gave a little curtsey. 'Thank you, kind sir. You're quite handsome yourself.' Her china-blue eyes gazed directly into his as she asked, 'Where shall we go then?'

Jim, still with her hand in his, answered, 'I thought I'd leave that to you. Where would you like to go?'

Mary took his arm as they walked, and an imp of mischief lurked behind the innocent eyes as she suggested, 'Well, we could go to Walsh's for dinner, and then there's a ballet on at the Montgomery Hall.'

Jim stared at her, half-believing. Then she spoilt the pretence by giggling, and Jim grinned and threatened her, playfully, 'You little devil, I'll put you over my knee and spank you in the same place that I pinched.'

'Oh, so you're one of those men that beat women!' She tossed back her head. 'I knew you were cruel.'

Jim, unused to girls, was flustered. Mary realised this and relented. 'I'm sorry, I was only joking. I came here because I liked being with you, not so that you could spend your money on me.'

As they walked on, arm in arm, she continued, 'I know, let's have a drink at Elliot's herbalists and then we can go down to that dance at the Labour Hall, it's only sixpence to go in.'

Jim pulled a handful of change out of his pocket and pretended to count it. He gave a slow grin. 'It's dear goin' out with girls, isn't it?' He turned to look at her. 'All right, we'll go, but you'll have to promise not to tread on my toes.'

Mary was indignant. 'You're awful, Jim Whiteley. It was *you* that trod on *my* toes at the wedding. I was crippled.'

'Yes, but you enjoyed it, didn't you?' At this point they reached the worn stone steps and entered the gloom of the shop. After a pint of sarsaparilla for Jim and an orangeade for his girl, they went on down to the Labour Hall. It wasn't anything grand, just a long, timber-framed room that was mostly used for meetings, although the spiritualists also met there to deliver messages from departed loved ones.

Tonight, though, it was dance night, and a pianist with a left hand like a seven-pound hammer, aided by a little old woman with a violin, churned out Valetas, Two-Steps and Lancers. Our young couple stumbled their way through the dances, and what Jim lacked in expertise, he made up for in energy.

Mary was swept off her feet by this son of Darnall, as they took the Gay Gordons by storm. During an interval, they sat with cups of tea and home-made cakes and Mary whispered, 'Tonight I told my dad I was going out with Isabel.'

Jim put a hand on his hip and primped his hair. 'Am I as nice-looking as Isabel?'

They both collapsed laughing, while serious devotees of the dance glowered disapprovingly. Jim and Mary, like all young lovers, were in a magic world where nothing could touch them.

The magic didn't fade, and at the witching hour of ten o'clock they walked up the hill to Darnall, still in the warm glow of first love. As Mary hugged his arm, Jim could feel through the sleeve of his jacket the pressure of one firm young breast, and the whole world was wonderful.

They reached Manterfield's chip-shop and Jim splashed out on fish and chips twice. They strolled on, juggling the hot chips in their mouths, the tang of hot vinegar stinging their nostrils. The fish was pure luxury. As a child, Jim had had to make do with a ha'p'orth of chips and scraps.

A light drizzle was falling as they climbed Handsworth Hill towards Oliver's Mount, but it went unnoticed. When they reached their destination they stood, only inches apart, and drank each other in with their eyes. Jim murmured, 'Thank you, Mary, it's been the greatest night of my life. I hope we can do the same next Saturday.'

For her part, Mary was more restrained and replied, 'You made it wonderful, Jim, thank you. I'll meet you in the same place.' She felt his hands on her shoulders and he pulled her towards him, to kiss her full on the lips. It was no expert kiss, and Jim's stubble didn't improve it, but Mary's blood raced. She whispered 'goodnight' and ran up the path, her face flaming. Neither of them noticed the curtain of the house twitch. He saw her turn at the door and blow him another kiss before it closed behind her and he was alone. He strolled home, oblivious to the rain.

★   ★   ★

The next time they met, Jim, still courteous, asked where she'd like to go.

'First of all, I'd like to see your pigs.'

Jim was flabbergasted. 'You can't go down there. You're a - a - woman!'

'Why can't I? Are you ashamed of them?'

'It's not that. They're mucky, an' you wouldn't believe the smell.' The full lips parted in a grin.

72

'Jim, lad, you ought to smell my dad's yard in summer when the raw hides have been stood for a few weeks. I'll bet it'll lick your pigs any day. Anyway, if you don't take me I'll go on my own. I bet they're only skinny little things.' She began walking down towards High Hazels Bottom. Jim ran to catch up. 'They're not, you know. Them pigs are gonna make me a lot o' money.'

'That's what I told my dad.' Her escort was horrified.

'You told your dad? Why for God's sake?'

'I had to tell him. My mother was looking through the window for me coming home and she saw you.' Her colour rose. 'She saw us when we ... said goodnight. They want me to take you home.' He was dumbfounded.

'What do they want to see *me* for? I 'aven't done owt wrong.' In his agitation, his dialect returned. Mary was demure and answered primly, 'They want to see if you're fit to associate with a little lady like me.'

Jim guffawed. 'A little lady? A girl who gets her bum pinched in pubs?'

She tossed her head haughtily. 'Jim Whiteley, you're vulgar, and I won't walk with you.'

He stifled his laughter and hurried to her side. 'What did you tell your mum and dad about me?'

Still with her nose in the air, Mary went on, 'I told them that you're a horrible boy who forced me to kiss him and pinched my ... bottom.' A delicious giggle exploded and she grabbed Jim's arm. 'No, I told them that you had your own business breeding pigs and that you're very clever. I told them all sorts of lies, I even told them that you're handsome.'

Jim grinned. 'I'm glad you tell the truth sometimes.'

At the sty, Mary was delighted with his livestock, and Jim treated her to a lecture on pig-rearing. The rest of the evening followed the pattern of the previous one, except that this time they kissed goodnight on the corner to avoid prying eyes.

★   ★   ★

In June of that year, the Armistice was signed, and this was the signal for the real celebrations to begin. The streets were festooned with flags and there were brass bands and street parties with a two-thousand-strong choir contributing their efforts to the general euphoria. Beer was in great demand, as people accepted that, at last, there was peace.

The next day, as Jim was returning from work, a crowd of kids were marching up the street singing,

Vote, vote, vote for Mester Johnson,
You can't vote for a better man,
If it's Johnson put 'im in,
if it's Browny chuck 'im out,
An' we'll put owd Browny in an owd tin can!

While they sang, with blithe disregard for the tune, they accompanied themselves by bashing bin-lids and saucepans. One even had a Boys' Brigade drum. These infant propagandists were paid by the Labour candidate in the municipal elections, who even now was making a last-ditch attempt to shore up a sagging minority. Mr Johnson was with them and went up to Jim, holding out a hand with a practised smile.

'Good afternoon, young man, and who do you think is going to win this election?' Their eyes were level as Jim answered thoughtfully,

'Well Mr Johnson, I 'ope you win, because it's time we 'ad somebody in the Town 'All that'll do somethin' for the workin' people. Then again, if I was old enough to vote, I'd want to know what you're goin' to do if *I* vote for you.' The candidate was a little taken aback by this formidable-looking youth but, gathering his wits, he launched automatically into his policy statement.

'I pledge that if I'm elected, I will not rest until we have improved the living standards of the downtrodden working classes. For too long the poorer people of this city have been deprived of proper education and good housing. Even now, we are pressing the council to start a building programme. We are supporting the unions in their fight for higher wages, and . . .'

Jim interrupted, 'What good are 'igher wages to a bloke who's dyin' of tuberculosis? 'Igher wages are no good to 'is wife an' kids when they're livin' on relief.'

Jim's voice was quietly emphatic as he went on, his tone hardening, 'If you look up now', and Johnson dutifully did so, 'you should be blinded by the sun, but the factories 'ave kindly given us a smoke-screen. Trouble is, we 'ave to breathe it all day, an' workin' blokes are dyin' of it. The bosses don't care about losin' a few men, 'cause there's plenty more growin' up to take their places.'

Johnson was openly admiring, and as Jim paused for breath, he said, 'Well lad, even though I don't agree with all you've said, I like the way you said it. How would you like to come to our meetings at the Labour Hall? We could do with one or two more like you in the Party. In fact, will you come for a drink with me now, I'd like to talk to you some more.'

Jim, though amazed at his own temerity, agreed, and they repaired to the *Wellington* where, over a pint, he enjoyed his first taste of politics.

Bill Johnson primed him. 'Take my tip, Jim, the first few meetings, just sit and listen until you get the feel of it. Not everybody can go on to get on the Council, but the Party need minds like yours, young minds as can look ahead' By the time they parted, Jim had agreed to attend the next meeting.

★   ★   ★

At their next tryst, on Saturday night as usual, Mary said, 'It's a lovely night, Jim, I think I'd like to go for a walk in the park.'

Jim agreed enthusiastically. They strolled arm-in-arm up the gravel path and finally came to rest on a seat near the bandstand. There they exchanged news of what had happened during the week. As the light began to fade and passers-by became less frequent, they kissed. Jim's technique had improved with practice, and they became quite absorbed.

During a break, when someone had intruded on their idyll, Mary announced, 'Oh Jim, I meant to tell you, my mum and dad said they'd like you to come to tea at our house tomorrow. They'd like to meet you.'

Jim groaned. 'Oh Gawd, I was afraid o' that.' He turned an imploring face. 'I don't have to, do I? I bet your dad's a funny bugger.'

Mary made a shocked face. 'Jim Whiteley! Swearing doesn't make you look big, it's the ignorant man's last resort.'

'Sorry, Mary, but I'm scared stiff o' meetin' 'em. I wouldn't know what to say. He's a gaffer an' I'm just an ordinary workin' bloke.'

'Well, what do you think my dad is? He still works for somebody else. Old Mr Eldon's *his* gaffer, and my dad works for a wage, same as you.'

Jim gave a rueful grin. 'All right, then, when do you want me to come?'

'We're having tea at six o'clock, and don't forget, you're in business for yourself.' She giggled. 'That puts you one up on my dad, for *you're* the gaffer.'

★   ★   ★

On Sunday afternoon Jim was dressed and ready by five o'clock and fidgeted with his handkerchief, tie, shoes, and anything else within reach. Joe was sitting with his paper and remarked, looking over his spectacles, 'What's up lad? Th'art like an ill-sittin' 'en. 'Enry Wilson's nowt special, ah knew 'im when 'e were a snotty-nosed kid wi' 'is trousers' backside aht. If it 'adn't been fer 'im bein' left some money by an uncle in Canada, 'e wun't 'ave 'ad two 'a'pennies to scratch 'is arse wi'. What money *tha's* got tha's 'ad ter work fer, so tha's nowt ter be ashamed on.'

After a last attempt to subdue his unruly locks by the application of lard, Jim, feeling like Danton on his way to the guillotine, set off for the abode of his beloved. Arriving at the house, which, graced by a bow window on the front seemed like a mansion to him, he stood for a moment to screw up his courage. He gave the toes of his boots a last rub on the back of his trouser legs and raised the knocker.

The summons echoed in the hall. Mary must have been waiting behind the door, for it opened immediately and her smile of welcome was balm to his soul. She looked over her shoulder, then jumped up on her tiptoes. He felt the pressure of her soft mouth and her perfume was in his nostrils.

She took him by the hand and led him into the parlour, where the table had been laid with a white damask tablecloth. In the centre was a vase of flowers. Mr Wilson, fully dressed in collar and tie, and wearing his jacket, rose from his easy chair near the fire and placed his pipe on the mantelshelf. Jim stepped forward, hand outstretched, and was gratified to find himself looking down on Mary's father. He saw a tubby little man with red cheeks and sporting a neatly-trimmed toothbrush moustache. Two brown eyes, squinched by a welcoming smile, twinkled at him from behind gold-rimmed bi-focals, and a light-coloured voice greeted him.

'Evening, Jim, welcome to the house.'

The lad took the chubby hand in his, gripping it warmly. 'Good evening, sir, I'm very pleased to meet you.'

Without releasing his grip, Mr Wilson exclaimed, 'My, you're a big un, Jim! Mary didn't tell me I'd need a box to stand on', and he chuckled as Mary's mother came in with a bread-plate in one hand, filled with slices cut corner to corner, and a bowl of trifle in the other. Jim was reminded of the Arabian proverb; 'If you would know your love, look at her mother', and in this case he liked what he saw.

Mary's mother placed the burden on the table and wiped her hands on her apron before shaking hands and saying as she smiled up at him, 'You're right, Mary, he *is* good looking.' She laughed as Jim's colour rose, then continued, 'Sit down and make yourself at home'.

Gratefully, Jim sank into one of the easy chairs beside the fire, as Mr Wilson claimed the other. Mary disappeared into the kitchen with her mother. After lighting his pipe, Henry Wilson beamed at Jim through a haze of smoke. 'I've heard you're a pigman, Jim. It's a good line to be in. Where do you sell 'em?'

Jim, still hesitant, replied, 'Up to now, sir, I've sold 'em at Armitage's pork butchers.'

Henry pointed his pipe at him. 'In future, I might be able to get you a better price up at the Shambles, and for goodness sake, don't call me "sir". My name's Henry, most people call me Harry.'

Jim loosened up. 'I haven't got any pigs ready yet, they're only nine months old, but I'll keep it mind. I've got eight, three boars and five sows, an' I might be breeding with some of 'em.' He found Mary's father easy to talk to, and they were deep in conversation when Mary and her mother came in with plates of cold lamb and salad.

Mary, relieved at the way Jim had been received, said, 'Come on, you two and get your tea.' Everyone took their places at the table and the talk continued disjointedly as Mary's parents tried to get to know this tall young man who had come into Mary's life. When tea was over, Mary's mother, Jane, after a lot of persuasion, sat down to the upright piano with the candle brackets on the front and played some popular songs, while the others joined in.

At nine o'clock, Jim excused himself on the grounds that he had to get up early and Mary walked with him as far as the corner of the street. They stood under the gaslamp, face to face, Jim with his hands on Mary's slender waist. He asked her how she thought he'd done. She placed her hands on his shoulders and their eyes met.

'I think my mother's fallen in love with you. She said that if she'd met you before my dad, you'd have been my father.'

Jim, the devil in his eyes, answered, 'Well, she *is* nice-lookin', and I bet *she* wouldn't tread on my toes.'

Mary glared art him in mock indignation. 'Jim Whiteley, I'll . . . ' and his mouth covered hers as his arms pulled her close. It was her first kiss of passion and it seemed to last forever as her hands locked behind his neck and her body moulded itself to his.

An eternity later they broke and she looked up, eyes shining. 'Jim, that was heaven'.

'I think I love you, Mary', he replied, and once more their lips met and they were back on the roller-coaster. A quarter of an hour later, after a last lingering kiss, they parted. As Mary walked home, a little unsteadily, her whole body was tingling with strange new forces. She paused before going in, afraid that there must be some outward sign of her trip into paradise.

★　　★　　★

On his first visit to the Darnall Labour Hall, Jim was all at sea as the jargon made the proceedings difficult to follow. As he left he was joined by Bill Johnson, who had failed to get elected onto the Council. The Labour man gave Jim his first of many lessons on procedure until 'Mr Chairman' and 'Proposed, seconded and carried' began to mean something to the budding politician. Reaching the terminus they went for the statutory pint, over which Jim's knowledge of the Labour Party was improved.

His education took another forward leap when, on his fourth visit, Bill, whom he thought of as his friend, was standing on the rostrum. Bill was outlining, and passing off as his own, some of the ideas that Jim had broached over a pint after one of the meetings. A couple of times Jim stood up to voice his opinions and heads turned as the vibrant, almost gravelly tones filled the hall.

John Cartwright, whom Jim still visited, remained at this time a valuable tutor on the art of public speaking. He schooled him in breath control, how to vary the volume of his delivery, and how to leave pregnant pauses to emphasise crucial points.

During one particular meeting, Jim was delighted when the chairman asked, 'I wonder if Brother Whiteley has anything to say on this subject.' Jim surprised even himself by getting up and speaking to a rapt audience for ten minutes on education. The words seemed to flow coherently as he outlined, without preparation, his own ideas on current school methods. He sat down to applause and *Hear, hear*'s from the body of the Hall. Bill Johnson, up on the rostrum, looked as if he had bitten into an unripe lemon, and Jim realised that far from being friends, they were fast becoming opponents. Time after time their ideas clashed, but increasingly Jim found that the support was going his way.

One day, the chairman came to him in the interval with a request. 'Look, Jim, we're havin' a division meetin' down at Carbrook Hall, an' we'd like you to come along and help represent Darnall Ward.' Jim chuckled. 'Don't be daft, Charlie, what would I talk about?'

'Just tell 'em what we're doin' down here. Tell 'em what we're tryin' to do in housin', education and so on. You know what you were sayin' about wantin' a hospital down this end You can do it. Apart from anythin' else, it'll be a good experience for you.'

Jim was doubtful. 'I don't know, Charlie, I'll think about it.'

'Well, it's not for a fortnight, so let me know next week. At a pinch I could get Bill Johnson to do it but . . .' He shrugged, his expression speaking for him.

As Jim walked home, his brain was buzzing with the knowledge that this was the chance to exercise his talent. At home, he started to set down his speech. He continually changed words, or the phrasing, and tried it out in his bedroom, but after half-a-page it sounded wooden and contrived. After three false starts, he abandoned it and contented himself with a detailed list of the subjects he wished to cover.

Mary had followed his progress with interest, and when he told her about his public speaking debut, she was really excited. 'That's wonderful, Jim, this is your chance.'

She hugged his arm, as they strolled through the park in the evening sunshine. 'Just imagine', she mused, and after a pause, she announced, in the manner of a toast-master, 'Ladies and gentlemen, I wish to present you your new Lord Mayor, James Henry Whiteley'.

Jim laughed uproariously. 'Gi' me a chance, Mary love, I might get chucked off the stage.'

They were just passing the bandstand when the girl exclaimed, 'Here you are, Big Jim, there's nobody about, so I'll be your audience. I'll sit here and you can try your speech on me.'

At first Jim demurred, but after looking around for intruders, he agreed. He had the speech notes with him, as he'd been planning to show them to Mary anyway, so he placed them on the rail of the bandstand and began.

'Brothers', and his voice rang out. Gazing down at Mary, he added with a smile, 'And Sisters. I am nobody special. Young I may be, inexperienced, yes, but I care deeply about what happens to my city, and I belong to the generation that will have to work and play in this industrial relic.'

He went on, carried forward on the wave of his own rhetoric, unaware that his audience now also consisted of late strollers attracted by the resonant baritone. Eventually, he noticed their presence, but after a slight stumble, he rallied and carried on to the end. The score or so people watching applauded the young man with the hypnotic voice.

As he climbed down from the stand he saw that Mary was giggling uncontrollably, and after an initial bout of indignation he was also infected. By the time their mirth had subsided, the crowd had cleared and the girl became serious.

'I was only laughing at those people, Jim, honestly. They didn't know what had hit them. Your speech was magnificent, and if you could hold those people's attention, you should be terrific speaking to Party members. You even had *me* listening to every word.'

Walking back through the gathering dusk with their arms around each other, Mary, who had found she could fit comfortably under Jim's left arm, looked up under arched brows and said, wonderingly, 'I was joking when I said that you might be Lord Mayor, but after that speech, I'm beginning to wonder.'

Jim bent and kissed her forehead. 'Don't let anyone hear you talking like that or they'll send round the green van.'

She peeped up at him again. 'Mark my words, Jim Whiteley, one of these days . . .' He stopped her with a kiss, his left hand moving gently to cup one firm breast. Gently, if reluctantly, Mary removed his hand and broke the kiss, warning him, 'Big Jim, you're trespassing again.'

He grinned widely. 'You can't blame me for tryin'. It's like owning a spice shop and not bein' able to pinch a toffee.'

The girl twisted her face into a mock ferocious scowl. 'Listen, son, *I* own the sweet shop, and you're getting only the spice you're entitled to until you buy it.' Then she whispered, 'And I hope it won't be too long, darling'. Once again, their lips met.

*　　*　　*

John Cartwright was pleased to see his young friend, and when Jim told him about the speech, he was delighted. 'I knew you had it in you. Have you anything prepared?'

Jim pulled out his notes. 'I tried writing out a proper speech, but it was no good, it sounded like a recitation. Then the other night . . .' and he went on to tell John about the incident at the bandstand.

Cartwright gave a deep, appreciative chuckle. 'Right, Mr Whiteley, may we have an audition?' He took a notebook and pencil and sat back expectantly. The youth started, a little hesitantly, but was soon in full spate as John watched, occasionally making notes. He ended with a flourish and Cartwright applauded gravely.

'Bravo, my young friend, I'm proud of you. I may have guided you, but yours is the talent, you're a natural orator. With someone of your background, I should have said that you'd have found great difficulty in finding a use for your gift, but me of little faith! You have found your niche, and I wish you success. However, there are a few minor improvements I could suggest.' He went through his notes, proposing a difference in emphasis here, soft-pedal that passage, change the wording of this phrase, and stress *this* part heavily.

He ended, 'And don't forget, Jim, not too much high-flown language, you are one of the people'.

'Thanks. Your opinion matters more than all the applause the other night at the bandstand.' As they talked, Jim noticed again the signs of age in his mentor. The long artist's fingers trembled as he drank his tea, he was reluctant to get up from his chair, and his skin, like yellowed silk, revealed the tracery of blue veins beneath. And now a full understanding of John's mortality struck, that sooner or later his aging body would fail, and the vast store of knowledge behind the high, domed forehead would be lost as the light went out of those compelling eyes.

With a conscious effort, Jim pushed the thought back into the depths of memory, to the same place that he consigned his fear of spiders, the time he killed the starling with his catapult, and the myriad other nasty things that he didn't wish to remember.

He forced himself to continue the conversation. Feeling oddly guilty, he was almost glad to escape into the open air, but the thought of John's death kept sneaking past the barrier that he had erected. By the time he reached home, however, Jim's young mind had come to terms with it and could consider it with equanimity.

Chapter Ten

J IM WAS BUSY in the sty with the brush and shovel when Ralph popped his head over the gate. 'Mornin', Jim, ow's things, lad?'

'Not bad, I managed to cure that rash that t'sows 'ad got.'

The older man tapped the dottle out of his pipe on the wall and continued, 'Aye, ah telled thee that stuff would shift it. Ah swear by it.' He started repacking the pipe and went on, "Ow'r tha goin' on dahn at t'Labour 'all?'

'I'm doin' all right. I'm goin' to make a speech at t'Divisional meetin' at Carbrook Hall next Thursday.'

'Oh aye?' Ralph lit his pipe and continued with a straight face. 'I were talkin' ter Bill Johnson t'other day. 'E works at that scrapyard on t'Cliffe.' He puffed appreciatively. "E were sayin' there' were a new lad in t'party, says 'e's a right jumped-up little bastard, too big fer 'is boots.'

Jim scraped a boot on the top of the shovel blade and replied, equally deadpan, 'Oh aye? I wonder who that can be.' He scraped the other boot. 'Well, you know Bill, 'e worries a lot. Must 'ave somethin' to do wi' losin' t'election'

The imperturbable Ralph tamped his pipe with the flat of the matchbox. 'As far as Bill's concerned, this new bloke's as welcome as an 'ore at a christenin'.' They both burst out laughing. 'Seriously Jim, if ah were you, ah'd watch me back, yer liable ter find summat stickin' in it. Bill can be a right bugger when 'e sets 'is stall aht. 'E dun't like anybody ter rub 'is nose in it.'

'Honest, mate, we haven't had a wrong word, but thanks for the warning.'

'It's not on'y 'im yer've ter watch aht fer.' He emphasized his words with the stem of his pipe. "E's thick wi' t'Oward brothers, an' yer know what a bleedin' family they are.'

Jim shrugged it off. 'That's all right, Ralph, I can 'andle meself.' Deep inside though, he knew that he could be in trouble. He was big, and nobody grew up in Darnall without fighting for something, but the Howard brothers, Cyril and Andy, were experienced street-fighters. They used fists, boots, or anything else they could lay their hands on. They'd been heard to brag that they'd 'kicked a copper all t'way from t'*Ball Inn* ter t'terminus', and Andy's speciality was to 'stick t'nut on'.

Ralph pointed once more with his pipe. 'Just thought ah'd mark yer card fer yer, mate', was all Ralph said as he left. That evening, Jim told Charlie Bowers, the local Party chairman, that he'd prepared his speech, though he was conscious as he did so of the smouldering fury in the eyes of Bill Johnson.

It was October in 1920 and Carbrook Hall was full as Jim mounted the platform with five other stalwarts of the East End wards, and for the first time he
doubted his ability to hold this audience of hard-headed steelmen. Two other
speakers preceded him, good, honest men, yet lacking the fire needed to com-
mand attention, and he noticed some talking and fidgeting in the front ranks.
When his turn came to speak, he rose, his notes on the table, and felt a return
of his misgivings. Then he recalled Cartwright's advice: 'Impose your will on
them'.

Turning to the chair, he began, 'Mister Chairman', then, to the expectant
faces below, 'Brothers'. The vibrant baritone was a call-to-arms, stirring the
blood, and he sensed the atmosphere change as he continued in a descending
tone. 'I am . . . nobody special.' He was humble, self-deprecating as he went on,
and he knew instinctively that he had them in the palm of his hand. He was
soon into his stride, carrying the hall on the tide of his enthusiasm. A third of
the way through his speech, his eye caught movement in the hall. It was Johnson, slinking away to lick imaginary wounds, and Jim forged ahead with
renewed vigour.

It was a new, triumphant Jim who finally concluded, 'Your leaders', indicating his fellow-speakers, 'cannot do it alone. They must have the whole-hearted
support of everyone in this hall. Nothing will be handed to you on a plate, you
will have to fight every inch of the way, but together we can make the Labour
Party a power to be reckoned with in this great city of ours.' He sat down and
shuffled his papers.

Long seconds of silence were suddenly broken as the audience rose to its
feet, and there was a storm of applause that only abated when the chairman
rose and held up his hands for order.

'Brothers, I think I speak for all of us when I say thank-you to Big Jim
Whiteley for a great speech, and I must say that I agree heartily with all he said.
Now we have Sam Barton from Brightside Ward to add his report to the proceedings', and he led the applause for the next speaker. Sam rose, and in a rueful tone, started,

'Good evenin' brothers. I don't know how I can foller a speech like that, but
I'll do my best.' He went on to tell the hall what was happening in the heavily-
industrialised area that was misnamed Brightside. There, the only greenery to
be seen was on the banks of the sad, polluted Don. The sun only shone on Sundays.

When the meeting ended, Jim came down from the dais and a stockily-built
man with grey hair cut *en brosse* and piercing grey eyes under beetling brows
came and shook his hand, saying decisively, 'Jim, thank you. That was one of
the finest speeches I've heard in many a long day. Where did you learn to use
words like that?'

Jim, not knowing whom he was speaking to, said truthfully, 'A friend of mine who used to be a lecturer taught me all I know.'

'If you don't mind me asking, what's the name of your friend?'

'He's a wonderful old man called John Cartwright.' The stocky man's face lit up and he exclaimed,

'I thought I detected John's influence. I once heard him give a lecture on economics, and an audience of working men gave him a standing ovation. Remember me to him when you see him and tell him he's done a good job on you. I've got to go now, but, congratulations, and I'm sure you'll go far.' Charlie Bowers, tall and loose-limbed, came across and, after praising Jim for doing a good job, asked, 'What did Albert 'ave to say to you?'

'Oh, he said I'd made a good speech, an' that I should go far. Who is he, any-how?'

Charlie chuckled. 'On'y Albert Taylor, t'leader o' t'Sheffield Labour Party. If he takes an interest in you, you're made.'

As he boarded the Darnall tram at the corner of Broughton Lane, Jim's head was buzzing with the compliments and the back-slapping. When the euphoria had subsided, his mind harked back to the way Johnson had deserted the meet-ing and to Ralph's foreboding, and by the time he disembarked at Ronald Road, he had the intrusive feeling that something nasty was happening.

He was passing the front of Taylor's shop when a hand came out and grabbed his arm. He was already on edge, so he managed to pull free and spin round, fists cocked, ready to lash out. Then he heard a deep chuckle, and a voice said, 'What's up Jim, did tha think it were t'Owards?'

'Bloody 'ell, Ralph', he exclaimed in relief. 'Y'ad me worried.'

'Ah were 'angin' abaht waitin' fer yer. Thought yer might like a pot in t'Lib-eral Club. Yer won't regret it.' There was an undercurrent of tension in his voice that made Jim follow the man without demur. They went up Irving Street to the club, and as they sat down in a quiet corner, the older man opened the conversation.

'Ah never told yer, Jim, but when ah were younger, ah were a bit of a tear-away, an' ah'd got some rough mates. T'other night, ah were in t'*Britannia*, near wheer t'Owards 'ang aht, an' I asked a few questions, abaht them an' Bill John-son. Somebody 'eard 'im makin' arrangements wi' 'em. Ternight they were waitin' in your entry, but ah sent a coupla lads ah know. One o' 'em'll come from t'top o' t'entry, an' t'other one o'er t'back wall, an' trap 'em between. They'll gi' 'em a good talkin' to.' He gave a slow grin. 'I 'ad a word wi' yer dad, an' they've gone for a drink.'

This underworld justice was alien to Jim. He started to say disapprovingly, 'It's good o' yer Ralph, but ah don't think . . .'

Ralph broke in. 'Look son, ah know yer big, an' yer've got guts, but these boys really play rough. It'd 'ave been knuckledusters an' lead pipe. Ah weren't gonna let yer finish up in 'ospital fer a shithouse like Bill.' He gave a short bark of laughter. 'They'll be 'avin' a word wi' 'im as well. Ah don't think yer'll 'ave any more trouble.'

They sat and talked, and he saw Ralph in a new light as this quiet, middle-aged man revealed a little of his mis-spent youth. Leaving the club, Ralph paused to speak to two chunky blokes at the bar, one of whom was sucking a knuckle. Jim heard him say as he left them, 'Awreight, thanks lads, ah owe yer a favour. Tara', and he rejoined his young friend as they went out into the night.

When he arrived home, Joe was sitting with a pot of tea and a plate of bread and dripping. As his son came in, he mumbled through a mouthful of dripping cake, 'Pour thissen some tea lad, there's some in t'pot.' He carried on munching. Jim sat down opposite his father and asked, 'You knew about this, didn't you, Dad?'

'Aye, 'e told us abaht it, an' I agreed wi' 'im. It were t'on'y thing ter do. T'Owards 'ave asked fer all they got. As far as th'art concerned, tha knows nowt abaht it', and he carried on with his supper.

★   ★   ★

The weeks went by, and Jim found himself more and more involved with the Labour Party, which was steadily increasing its support across the City. Instead of being just a spectator, he was taken under Charlie Bowers' wing and pushed into serving on committees. He helped to fill the gap left by Bill Johnson, who, since the Carbrook Hall meeting, had hardly been seen. Bowers lent him books on the Labour Party and Jim, ever the avid reader, studied them from cover to cover.

One evening, Albert Taylor had been speaking at a meeting, and in the interval he came across to Jim who was sitting drinking tea. Albert, astride the wooden bench with cigarette in hand, spoke at length.

'I've been wantin' to get hold of you, Big Jim He paused, then rolled the name around his tongue. 'Big – Jim – Whiteley. Yes, I like it. What I wanted to say is that since the war ended, there are few jobs in the steel industry, and I'm afraid the workin' bloke's goin' to get a rough deal. On the other hand, this is the time – I mean in the next couple of years – when we can build the Labour Party into a powerful force in Sheffield. Now's the time to make it a Labour Council. The Tories, the Churchmen and the City Fathers have had it their way long enough. The Firths, the Cammells and their kind must be forced to release their stranglehold on the city.'

He paused, and Jim interrupted, 'Stranglehold is the right word, Mister Taylor. These big steel bosses *are* strangling the working population with the smoke that they belch out of their chimneys, all in the name of money.' Taylor listened approvingly as Jim rode his favourite hobby horse.

'That's good, Jim, that's the sort of thing we've got to concentrate on. Anyway, in the months ahead I want you to really work at it, get to know the union leaders, go into the clubs and get your face known. For the time being, this is between you, me and Charlie Bowers. Charlie knows that he hasn't got it in him to be a councillor, but both he and I know that you're the best man we've got for t'Darnall Ward. But you need to get the background. When people ask you questions, you have to have the answers ready, whatever the subject. It'll be hard work, but remember, Chuck and me are behind you all the way – and for Christ's sake', with an engaging smile, 'call me Albert!'

Jim replied in kind. 'Thanks a lot, Albert. And for Christ's sake, call me Jim.' They both laughed.

Jim hurried home to tell his parents about it, the words tumbling in their haste to get out. When his son had run out of breath, Joe got up from the chair and took his hand, not shaking it, just the warm grip of one man to another whom he recognizes as his equal.

He said in a voice which had a suspicion of a quaver, 'Jim lad, tha's made me proud ter 'ave thee as a son, an' ah think tha might be t'first un ter mek t'Whiteley name famous.' He swallowed hard and continued. 'An' if tha's got Albert Taylor at thi back, th'art 'alfway theer. 'E's 'ad ter tek a lot o' stick feightin' fer t'workin' man, 'e even 'ad ter go dahn t'spike fer it. Best o' luck, son.'

Alice kissed her son's bristled cheek, looked up at him and murmured, 'You were reight ter tell me not ter call yer Jimmy, it *were* a babby's name, weren't it?' She squeezed his biceps and pride glowed in her soft brown eyes.

★　　★　　★

With his latest news bursting to be told, Jim was knocking on Mary's door at half-past-six. Jane came to the door, her face lighting as she saw who it was.

'Come in, Jim, Mary'll be down in a minute.' Closing the door, she added, 'Do you mind coming into the kitchen? Henry's having ten minutes in the parlour.' She bustled into the tiny kitchen.

Jim was sat with a cup of tea when Mary came downstairs, her blond bob sleek and shining. She sat on the arm of his chair.

'Right then, Jim, what is it? Can't you live without me till the weekend?' She leaned over and kissed him on the forehead; her blue eyes danced.

'Mary!' her mother exclaimed with mock reproof, then her expression softened. 'I'll go and see if your dad's awake', and she disappeared in the direction of the parlour. Seizing the opportunity, Mary bent over. Her lips found his and clung, as he breathed in the warm girl-smell of her. They embraced again and Jim was breathless.

'Listen, you little witch, before your mother comes back.' The girl jumped up and struck a pose with her arm across her forehead.

'He spurns my love, then casts me off like an old shoe.' Then, serious, 'What do you want to tell me?'

'They're putting me up as Labour candidate for t'Darnall Ward on t'Council, and Albert Taylor says I stand a good chance of gettin' on.' As an afterthought, 'In a few months, I mean'. Mary was delighted.

'That's grand, love.' She twirled round and asked, 'Do you think I'll make a good Lady Mayoress?'

Jim made a face. 'Don't talk daft, I haven't got a big belly.' Then he changed the subject. While I'm here, I want to ask your father if we can get engaged.' Mary, flabbergasted, flopped in the other chair and her lips formed the word 'engaged', but no sound came out. She dropped to the carpet and rested her elbows on her boyfriend's knees. Her eyes were bright as she gazed up at the serious-faced youth and breathed, 'Do you mean it, love? Do you *really* want to marry me?' Her smooth forehead crinkled in disbelief.

Jim took her hands and said gravely, 'It's the thing I want most in all the world'. Then, in a lighter vein, 'Anyroad, it's me that's supposed to kneel down, not you'.

This was the tableau as Jane and Henry walked in. Mary ran and kissed her mother while Jim stood feeling self-conscious. He cleared his throat and said to Henry in a formal voice, 'Mr Wilson, I'd like to get engaged to your daughter.'

The little man, his spectacles on the end of his nose, stared in amazement, then smiled and said, 'You ought to see yourself, son, you look like a bloke off one of Jane's sloppy books.' He stepped forward, hand outstretched, and continued, 'Course you can, Jim, I'd be proud to have you in the family. I only hope you don't mind having me for a father-in-law.' They shook hands, Henry's glasses bouncing precariously.

Mary burst out, 'That's not all, Dad, Jim looks like being a Labour councillor.' Henry sat down and took out his pipe.

'Well, it's a night for surprises', and he looked up at Jim with a sly grin. 'I suppose you know I always vote Tory?' The lad nodded mutely, apprehensive. Henry continued, 'Do you support Wednesday or United?'

'Er, Wednesday?' Jim was hesitant, as Henry lit his pipe. 'That's all right then, a Wednesdayite can't be all bad', and he laughed, Jim joining in, the atmosphere suddenly festive.

★   ★   ★

When Jim had finished his round on Saturday he dashed home, and after a quick change was on his way to the terminus to catch a tram. The juggernaut rattled and clanged its way down Staniforth Road, on its way to Sheffield, the bell warning pedestrians as it swung left at Staniforth Road Junction. The driver in his heavy gloves stamped on the pedal and the brakes struck sparks from the rails.

Getting off in the Wicker, he made his way to the pawnshop where he knew he could find a selection of rings, unclaimed pledges from some unlucky borrowers.

The proprietor was glad to show Jim his stock, and dry-washing his hands humbly, asked, 'Has Sir any preference? Diamonds? Rubies? Sapphires?' Jim spread his hands expressively. 'What can we show you?' After inspecting about fifty rings, some as dear as ten pounds, which in those days was more than seven weeks' wages, he chose one with a central sapphire surrounded by diamonds. It cost him two guineas after knocking the shopkeeper down from two pounds ten, and he even got a fancy box thrown in.

On the stroke of seven o'clock he was outside Cheetham's on the terminus waiting impatiently for his lady-love. When he saw her approach, he hurried to meet her. They walked arm-in-arm for a while, but soon he couldn't contain himself any longer.

'I've got something for you. I went to town and bought it this morning.' He took out the little leather box and handed it to her. As Mary opened it, he continued, 'I picked it to match your eyes'. For the first time since he'd known her, he saw tears roll down her cheeks.

He bent over her, concern showing on the rugged features. 'What is it, Mary? What have I said?'

She gazed up at him, eyes misty, and her voice was husky. 'Silly old Jim, you couldn't do anything wrong. I'm just happier than I've ever been in my life.' Raising herself on tiptoe she kissed him and whispered, 'Thank you, darling, it's wonderful. Now put it on for me.'

She held out her left hand. Jim placed the ring on her third finger and she hooked her hand through his right arm, careful to see that the ring was in plain view. When they reached the corner opposite the 'Iron Duke', Mary asked, 'Where are we going then? Dancing?'

'I'd like to show Mum and Dad your new ring, and I want you to meet them again. The last time you saw them was at Sally's wedding.'

'Right, love, but does your mother know we're coming? We don't want to surprise her, you know what mothers are.'

'That's all right, I warned 'em.' He hugged her arm. 'They might go out and leave us alone.'

Joe and Alice welcomed Mary warmly, and the ring was duly admired. Joe remarked, 'Ah were wonderin 'ow long it'd take this idiot son o' mine to propose. Ah knew you were t'one at Sally's weddin', an' ah don't think either on yer coulda found anybody better.'

Alice followed with, 'It'll be nice 'avin' another daughter, an' if 'e doesn't be'ave 'imself, come an' tell me.'

The tea was poured and they sat and chatted. At nine o'clock Joe stood up and stretched. 'I 'ope yer don't mind, Mary, but we said we'd go down ter t'*Bradley* fer t'last hour. Still', he added with a slow smile, 'ah suppose yer'll find summat ter occupy yer time'.

Jim grinned and Mary blushed prettily. The old couple were soon away, leaving the young lovers to their own devices, and Jim was quick to take full advantage of his opportunity.

★   ★   ★

The prospective Labour candidate dived into his work with a will, still on his favourite hobby horse – the smoke problem. He visited doctors and hospitals, talked to furnacemen, hammer-drivers and press operators, and read all he could get on chest complaints. Odd times, he would go to Council meetings with Taylor as a visitor to get the feel of the Council chamber.

When Albert asked him for his impressions, Jim replied, 'To tell you the truth, it made me feel inferior with all those important people.'

'You call those people important? I'm not, and I'm a councillor. The important people are out on the streets and in the factories. *They're* the ones you'll be asking to vote for, Jim. It's *their* money that you'll be spending in the Council chamber. I know some of the fat-gutted Tories in there think that it's their own money they're throwin' around. If they do anything for anybody, it'll be for the ten percent with ninety percent of the money. It needs more of *our* class in there, so that we can do more for the other ninety percent of the population that has to make do with what's left. Our target is a Labour council and a Labour government.'

Jim had been looking thoughtful. 'What gets up my nose, Albert, is the way they talk about people as if they're, well, cattle. It's no good puttin' that lot in good housin', they say, they wouldn't appreciate it, or if we do away wi' them three streets, it'll be just right for a factory. Nothin's said about people havin' feelin's. An' – an' what about the old people? You can't move a sixty-year-old tree without killin' it, its roots are too deep.' Albert put his arms round Jim's shoulders as they walked across Surrey Street towards the tram stop in Fitzalan Square.

'I can see your point, friend, but its hard to strike a balance between stagnation and progress, and, sadly, you can't make omelettes wi'out breakin' eggs.'

Jim's face took on stubborn lines, the bottom lip thrust out and the muscles knotting on the jawline. He walked on in silence for a few yards, then blurted, 'Did you hear yourself? *You're* at it now. People aren't eggs, an' them terraces aren't eggboxes, they're homes, only one up an' one down, but to the people who live in 'em, they're home. Why not build a factory up at Broomhill, an' shift *them* into new houses on this side of town?'

Albert looked at him quizzically, then chuckled and slapped him on the back. 'That's my boy, make 'em have it.' Even Jim had to laugh at his own vehemence. Taylor continued. 'Save it mate, save it. Soon you'll be a councillor. I've an idea that when Big Jim talks they'll have to listen. Still, I must admit you've got a good argument. Would you like to tell me about it over a pint?'

Jim's jaw lost some of it's belligerent thrust and he grinned. 'Sorry, Albert, I get carried away. How about a pint in t'*Adelphi*? T'beer's good, an' we might see some chorus girls from t'*Lyceum*.'

★   ★   ★

One day, as usual, after his milk round, Jim turned Bonny in the direction of Manor Farm and gave the mare her head. He swung into the yard and came to a stop opposite the stable. He unharnessed the grey and led her into the stall to give her a rub down with dry straw before going into the dairy to swill the churns. He took the money-bag to the farmhouse and knocked.

The door opened and Ivy, her hands covered in flour, said, 'Come in, lad. Mash us a cup o' tea, t'kettle's on.' He dropped his burden on the scrubbed deal table and went to where the kettle was boiling on the hob. He was scalding the leaves in the big brown teapot when he turned round and saw George lying on the sofa, his face drawn, leaden under the tan.

'What's up, George, are you poorly?'

The man's smile was weak, his voice reedy. 'Aye, son, ah'm a bit rough, ah've 'ad one or two o' these dos lately.' His breathing was fast and shallow. 'Doctor Shaughnessy says 'e thinks ah've got sugar, so ah've got ter tek it steady an' watch what I eat. T'trouble is, ah've got t'farm ter run, an' owd 'Erbert can't do it. 'E can't see ter t'calvin', an' ah've got two beasts in calf.'

The sick man took the pint pot from Ivy and sipped the scalding tea. 'Ah've been laid 'ere studyin', an' ah've decided, ah'll 'ave ter tek yer off t'milk round.'

As Jim's face fell, he said, 'No, what ah mean, ah'd like yer ter come in full-time an' 'elp me ter run t'farm'.

Jim was torn between delight and doubt. 'I'm glad you made t'offer George, but I don't know if I can do it.'

'Look lad, you've done t'afternoon milkin', an' you 'elped me when Betsy calved. Ah think yer a born farmer. If yer do awreight, ah'll mek yer a partner, an' we'll share t'profits. Until yer prove yerself ah'll pay yer three quid a week. Ah suppose yer'll need it if yer gerrin' wed.'

'Thanks ever so much, I won't let you down.' Then, as an afterthought, 'I'll have to get shut o' my pigs though'.

The farmer smiled tiredly. 'Ah've thought o' that as well. Yer know that little stone-built barn at t'bottom o' t'long field? Ah think yer could use that fer 'em, an' yer could keep an eye on 'em while yer workin'.'

The lad was overjoyed. 'That'll be great, George, when do I start?'

'Finish this week aht, an' we'll get a lad ter do t'milk next week. Ah've got me eye on a good un.'

Walking home through the fields, Jim couldn't believe his luck. Three pounds a week would be untold wealth. His father, who'd had to take a job as a timekeeper because of his chest, was on much-reduced money. Now he could slip him the occasional quid. To this son of Darnall, the last few days had been a dream come true. The gods were smiling.

★   ★   ★

For the first few weeks, Jim was working from dawn to dusk at the farm, but as George's health improved, his burden lightened and he could find the time to continue his political activities. Mary began going to meetings with him, applauding wildly when he spoke. She offered constructive criticism and helped him to keep his feet on the ground. Quite apart from the meetings, the young couple were spending more time together, a familiarity which bred content.

When George finally announced that he was making Jim a partner at the farm, even the conservative Mary began talking of an early marriage. However, Jane and Henry wanted them to wait until their daughter was twenty-one, which was twelve long months away. One night, when Jim came home, Alice noticed the lowered brows and the craggy set of the jaw. 'What's wrong, Jim? It's not like you to be bad-tempered.'

'Aw, it's Henry and Jane, they still say we have to wait while Mary's twenty-one. It's daft. I'm makin' more than most blokes, an' we've got a tidy nest-egg. They're just bein' bloody-minded. In March I'll be gettin' my first share from the partnership, we could have had a good weddin'.' He punched the cushion and bounced down in the chair, glowering. Joe was reading the *Star* as if he hadn't heard, but there was the ghost of a smile that had nothing to do with the last race at Catterick.

Alice tried to pour oil on troubled waters. 'I know 'ow you feel, son, but it's different for a girl. 'Er parents'll be scared of 'er doin' the wrong thing. They'll on'y 'ave 'er 'appiness at 'eart.'

Joe lowered his paper. 'Ah've been thinkin' Mother. We ought ter get together wi' 'Enry an' 'is missus.' Then, to Jim, 'Could yer mention it to 'em? Ah thought we could 'ave a drink at t'Liberal club. Tell 'em any night'll do.'

'All right', growled the disgruntled Jim, 'I'm goin' to bed'.

As he disappeared upstairs, Joe chuckled. 'Ah know what 'e's goin' through.' He took off his spectacles. 'Remember that night in 'Igh 'Azels Park when t'copper come an' stopped us. If 'e'd been ten minutes later . . .' and he left it in the air.

Alice bridled. 'Oh, Joe', and she blushed like a teenager.

Joe went on. 'Ah think ah'd better remind 'Enry o' when 'e were courtin'.'

'Please, love, don't get arguin', yer know 'ow yer get yer rag out when yer've 'ad some ale . . .'

Joe interrupted. 'Don't thee worry, Mother, ah've grown aht o' that.' He smiled enigmatically. 'Ah'll just 'ave a little chat wi' 'im, see if ah can change 'is mind.'

A week later, negotiations completed, there was a summit meeting at the Liberal Club. By seven o'clock Joe and Alice were ensconced in the lounge bar, dressed in their best. As Jane and Henry came in, Joe went to the bar and brought back a whisky and a port and lemon which he handed to his already-seated guests.

Henry beamed as he put down the drinks. 'Thanks very much, Joe, it isn't often I drink whisky, but I'm willin' to make an exception.'

Joe answered, 'Ah think we ought ter drink ter t'young couple's engagement, we 'aven't celebrated it yet. All the best to Mary and Jim.' He raised his glass and the others followed suit. Four drinks later the atmosphere had become quite convivial, with the pianist playing all the old favourites. Joe got up to go to the bar.

'Yer comin' ter gi' us a lift, 'Enry? Ah don't want ter spill any food.' Henry, chuckling, got to his feet, a little unsteadily. 'Yes, but before we do, I'll 'ave to go to t'back.'

'Aye, that's a good idea', said Joe, 'ah could do wi' one meself'. Making for the gents', he continued, 'It's nice ter see t'young people makin' plans, i'n't it?' He grinned at the little fat man. 'D'yer remember your young days? Yer were a bit of a lad when you lived on Irvin' Street.'

Henry, a bit bemused, muttered, 'Well, we all sowed our wild oats, didn't we?' and laughed a little uncertainly. They walked across the yard into the men's toilet, and as they relieved themselves, Joe asked, 'Whatever 'appened ter that lass yer were knockin' abaht wi' then?' What were 'er name? Irene Burgin, that's it! She went ter stop wi' er aunt in Woodhouse. She were badly or summat.'

Shamefaced, Henry answered, 'Her parents didn't like her goin' wi' me as she were only seventeen, so they separated us.'

'Oh, ah see. Mind yer, a mate o' mine were comin' out o' t'*Cross Daggers* theer, an' 'e saw 'er pushin' a pram.' He winked. 'Still, that's past 'istory, i'n't it? Least said, soonest mended. Yer've gorra good un theer wi' your Jane.'

They went back to the lounge, where Alice and Jane had got their heads together. They took fresh drinks to the table and sat down. Joe gave the ball a kick.

'Talkin' abaht Mary an' Jim, it's a pity ter keep 'em apart, they're gerrin' reight impatient, an' yer know 'ow young people are, they can't wait.' He gazed at Henry, his face inscrutable. Jane joined in.

'Yes, but we want to be sure they're right for each other.' Alice demurred, 'When me an' Joe'd on'y known each other for a month, ah knew 'e were t'on'y one fer me'.

Henry was uncomfortable under Joe's basilisk gaze. 'Well, Jane', he said, 'I tend to agree wi' 'em. It's only twelve months, isn't it, an' we don't want any accidents.'

His wife disagreed. 'No, Henry, I don't think so.' Then the worm turned.

'I think I know best, Jane', said Henry, and turning to Joe, continued. 'You're right, we'll let 'em get married when they want to.' Flustered, Jane retired from the contest, outvoted by three to one.

Alice informed them, 'Jim were sayin' 'e'll be gettin' 'is first payment from t'farm in March, an' they'd like to get married then. I 'ope it's awreight wi' you.'

Now that the thorny problem of the wedding was resolved, the stiffness went out of the evening, and by the time they parted on the terminus they were old friends. Joe and Alice strolled back towards Kirby Road, arm-in-arm. She smiled up at him and asked, 'What went on between you an' Henry when you went ter t'back. 'E looked as if 'e'd seen a ghost.'

Joe laughed out loud. 'Aye, 'e'd seen a ghost awreight lass – they called 'er Irene Burgin. Yer remember, she got 'ersen in t'puddin' club an' 'Enry were t'first favourite fer t'cup. Ah just mentioned it to 'im.'

Alice's brown eyes danced and she giggled. 'You crafty owd devil, ah didn't know yer were a blackmailer.'

Joe's grin was expansive. 'Oh, I 'ave me moments, Mother, an' it's t'least ah could do fer t'kids.' They walked on, still man and maid in spite of the long hard years of battle against the ever-present grinning spectre of poverty.

★　　★　　★

Once the news of the coming nuptials became common property, the happy couple began receiving contributions toward the bottom drawer – odds and ends of furniture, including a table and chairs from Henry and dressing table from Joe. Ralph weighed in with a set of cast-iron saucepans.

Jim had become a popular figure during his milkround, having delivered to most houses within a quarter-mile radius of the terminus, and miscellaneous articles were donated. The parlour and Jim's bedroom at number thirty-two Kirby Road became the repositories for an assortment of bric-a-brac. Some of the items, Mary insisted firmly, would not be needed in any house of hers.

February came, with more snow and still they hadn't found a suitable house anywhere nearby. One evening Jim arrived back from the farm and found his mother all agog.

She burst out, 'Ah was down at Elderkin's on t'bottom, today, an' owd Mrs Elmore from number thirty-eight was in theer. As she were comin' out, Mrs Elderkin said, "If ah don't see you again afore yer go, all the best". I asked Mrs Elderkin where t'owd lady were goin', an' she said she were goin' ter live wi' 'er daughter on t'Manor estate. Ah thought, yer could see t'rent man when 'e comes on Friday an' see if it's goin'.'

'That sounds like good news, Mam, but t'house'll want a good fettlin' before we can move in.'

'That's nowt', said his mother, 'ah'll help thee get it ready, an' it's a month ter t'weddin' '.

'I'll have a word with Mary about it, first. She might not like it, then I'd be in trouble.'

But Jim's fears were groundless, for when he told his fiancée about it, she was enthusiastic. 'It'll be grand, love. I'd sooner be near your mother than mine, she tries to treat me like a kid. Tell you what, I've seen some lovely wallpaper in Sheffield for the front room, an' we can distemper the kitchen a nice peach colour. There's another thing I'd like, love', she said, her voice wheedling. 'Could I have one of those new gas stoves? – I could cook you some lovely dinners.' When she saw his expression she added, 'Please, Jim'.

'Do you know how much they cost woman?'

'Yes, you pay for them through the meter. It won't cost us much.'

'Don't forget, we want lino, curtains an' rugs as well.' Her face fell and he relented. 'Go on, then, we'll rent one from t'Gas Company, but don't blame me if it blows up.' She jumped up and kissed him.

'Thank you, darling, it'll be lovely.'

Joe took his reward in the form of hugs and kisses, but he wanted more. Mary had been feeling more secure with Jim since she had been wearing his ring, and had allowed their courting to become more passionate. Still, with great self-control on her part, she denied him the big prize. At the last attempt, she had said in her warm husky voice, 'Look love, I want to just as much as you, p'raps more, but I'm sorry, I'm old-fashioned. I've been brought up to believe that it's the most precious thing I can give my man and I want it to be brand new for you. So please, please, be happy with what you've got, darling. It won't be long.'

Jim was contrite. 'Sorry, Mary, I've been stupid, I'll be patient.'

On the following Friday, when the rent-man called, Alice asked him about number thirty-eight. His face held the sad expression of a grieving basset hound, and his dewlaps shook as he considered the request.

'Ah don't know, Mrs Whiteley', he intoned in a doom-laden voice, 'ah've got other people on the waitin' list'.

'Yes, ah know that, but it's fer my son, 'e gets wed in three weeks. Yer've no need ter worry about yer money, 'e's got more comin' in than me an' Joe, an' we've never knocked yer.'

Mournfully, the collector fiddled with his book and turned to number thirty-eight, then sighed sepulchrally, 'Awright, then, but 'e'll 'ave ter pay the rent, even if 'e's not livin' in it. Missis Elmore's goin' next Friday so ah'll want me first week then.' He closed the book with a snap. 'See yer next Friday', and he disappeared up the entry, bowed like Atlas with the world on his shoulders.

★   ★   ★

As soon as they had the key, Alice and Jane descended on number thirty-eight and it was soon as clean as a hound's tooth. The floors were scrubbed white and the windows were sparkling and the outside lavatory was freshly distempered. Now Jim and Mary could start putting flesh on their dreams.

A week before the wedding, Jim found the time to visit the garden in the forest and found his friend a little under the weather. He invited the old man to the wedding but Cartwright's response was to shake his head slowly. The old pullover hung baggier than ever on the gaunt frame, but the light still flickered in the hooded eyes, although the lids seemed bruised.

'Thank you, Jim', he said, his voice subdued, 'but I'm not sure if I'll be able to come. I'm managing to get around here, but it's a long way to Darnall.' He held out his hand and the lad took it. 'In case I don't see you, I'd like to wish you and Mary a lifetime of happiness and . . . be kind to each other.'

After he had topped up John's supplies Jim started back toward the farm, the sad fronds of dried bracken crunching beneath his boots. He stopped to watch an anxious squirrel scrabbling for last year's missed acorns. High in the sycamores the rooks argued endlessly.

He arrived in time to relieve the swollen udders of his charges and put the new milk, foaming, through the separator, saving the cream for Ivy to make into butter. On the way to the house he called in at the pig-sty to look at Molly, one of the prospective mothers, who gazed at him with large liquid eyes as he inspected her distended abdomen.

'You're gettin' big, old girl. I hope you hang on 'til after March sixteenth. I've enough trouble with one woman.' He slapped the pig on the flank and crossed the yard to the farmhouse, where George greeted him.

'Hello, Jim, everythin' awreight?'

'Yes, they gave nearly four churns today.' Bolsover rubbed his hands. 'That's them new linseed cakes, they mek a difference, y'know.' Jim continued, 'I just had a look at Molly, I hope she doesn't drop it before t'weddin' '.

'She'll be awreight.' He picked up an envelope from the table and handed it to Jim saying, ''Ere y'are lad, yer first dividend – thirty-six quid.' Grinning at Ivy he added, 'If yer go upstairs an' look in t'front bedroom, yer'll find summat that might come in 'andy.'

A red-faced Jim came back downstairs carrying an old cradle, polished with age. George laughed like a drain as his grinning partner thanked him.

'Rushin' things a bit, aren't you? Mary might have somethin' to say about it.'

'Well, look after it, me grandad were rocked in that.' He became wistful. 'It's a pity *we* didn't get a chance ter use it.' He and Ivy exchanged glances.

'I'm sorry to hear that, George, but I'll put it to good use', and he changed

94

the subject. 'I hope you're not goin' to be late next Saturday with the gig. Don't forget, it's number seven, Oliver's Mount, at half-past-two.' George Bolsover looked ruefully at his wife .

'Yer see, Ivy, yer mek a man a partner, an' next thing yer know, 'e's dishin' orders out!'

★   ★   ★

The March of 1922 came in like a lamb and stayed that way, contrary to popular expectation.The spring sun bestowed his benediction as Jim and his father made their way to the church, yet there was the bite of late frost in the air. They were about to go in when Jim, looking in the direction of Mary's house, saw a tall, bent figure that he recognized. He ran down to meet John Cartwright, who was dressed in blue serge with a bowler on his grey head. Gone were the baggy old sweater and patched trousers, and the long jaw was clean-shaven. As Jim approached, his teacher rested on a silver-handled cane, his breathing laboured.

Taking the old man's arm, he exclaimed, 'I didn't recognize you, John, you're lookin' smart.'

Cartwright gave a tired smile, 'It must be ten years since I wore this suit, it's high time it saw the light of day again.' They walked up to the church where Joe was waiting. The man of letters and the man of toil eyed each other as Jim made the introductions, then their hands met. Joe's hand was broad with spatulate fingers, and the palm was cracked and calloused, whereas John's was a slim, artist's hand, the fingers long and tapering. They shook warmly. Joe spoke first.

'Between us, John, ah think we did a good job on 'im, but yer gi'en 'im more than I ever could.'

'No Joe, *you* built the man, I just added a little polish.' The prospective bridegroom looked at the two most important men in his life and remarked, 'When you've finished talkin' about me as if I was a drop-leaf table, don't you think we'd better get inside the church before Mary comes?'

Inside, Jim took his place beside a resplendent Ralph, who was best man. Despite his finery, there was still a faint aroma of pig.

Jim whispered anxiously, 'I hope you've got the ring safe.' Ralph grinned, showing crooked teeth worn to a gap by successive pipe-stems. He held up the ring on the first joint of his little finger, but as he tried to take it off, panic showed in his face.

In an agonised whisper he confided, 'Ah can't gerrit off, Jim, it's stuck.'

The priest, tall and forbidding, stood with Bible in hand and glared at them disapprovingly over his half-moon spectacles as Jim muttered out of the corner of his mouth, 'Spit on it an' have another go.'

Ralph put the digit in his mouth. It tasted so unpleasant that he made a face as he struggled to free the ring, confiding, 'I 'ad ter go an' lock t'pigs up on t'way 'ere.'

Jim stifled a nervous laugh as the recalcitrant gold band came clear, then the organ struck up with the wedding march.

Down the aisle, walking regally, came Mary, on the arm of her beaming father, and Jim's heart stopped. His womenfolk, with their handkerchiefs at the ready, all disappeared, as did the church and it's serried ranks of guests, and he saw only his love, as if in a halo of mist. Bemused, he thought, 'This isn't Mary, it's a goddess'.

As she approached, a stray ray of spring sunshine striking through the stained-glass windows dappled the rippling ivory satin of her gown with red, green and gold, and she appeared to walk on light. When the vision finally reached his side, she smiled radiantly through the cloud of her veil and this scruffy lad from Darnall knew he was the luckiest man in Sheffield.

From then on, for him, the entire ceremony went by in a blur. He answered the priest's questions as if in a trance, replying with a fervent 'I do' to the parson's 'Wilt thou take this woman?'.

The moment came to place the gold band on her finger. Then, as he lifted her veil, he was told, 'You may kiss the bride', and he did, tenderly and reverently. It was a proud man that walked back up the aisle, Mary on his arm. As they emerged, triumphant, there was a festival atmosphere on the terminus, as the inhabitants of the village cheered the young couple.

George was waiting with the shining gig, and a glossy Bonny, nostrils flaring, stamped impatiently in the shafts. Deferentially, Bolsover handed the bride into the vehicle and Jim followed. Then they were off to the reception at the *Duke of York*, the cheers of the onlookers ringing in their ears.

Mary preceded her new husband up the stairs of the pub and it was as if history repeated itself as Jim saw before him that beautifully curved area of ivory satin. In spite of himself, his hand moved of its own volition and his fingers applied pressure to a firm buttock, a little more gently than on that other memorable occasion. A laughing Mary turned and brandished the large bouquet of roses, exclaiming, 'Watch it, Jim, this bouquet's a lot bigger than last time, and it's got prickles in it.'

He cowered, pleading, 'No, Mary, not the flowers again.' They crossed the room toward the top table and he whispered, 'This time I'm going to have a look at your bruises', and Mary blushed like the roses.

The guests applied themselves to the victuals, and very soon the toasts were passed around. Ralph got to his feet to propose the health of the bride and groom, but bedlam reigned. Putting two fingers in his mouth, he gave an ear-splitting whistle and turned to Jim, an expression of distaste on his face.

'Ah, forgot again. It tastes rotten.' The hubbub subsided and he began. 'Ah don't know much abaht makin' speeches', and he took out a sheaf of papers, 'so ah'll keep it short'. There was a burst of laughter and he held up the papers. 'These are all bills.' He waited again for order. 'This lad 'ere, ah've known 'im fer nigh on twelve years, an' ah've never known 'im do anybody a bad turn. That's 'ow ah can't understand why 'e's inflicted 'isself on a lovely gentle lass like Mary. Ah don't know what 'e'll be like as a 'usband, but 'e's a bloody good pigman. Anyroad, ah want ter propose a toast ter two real nice people.' He held up his glass. 'Jim and Mary'.

The guests drank the toast, and he continued, 'An' now we'll 'ear a word from t'owd man', and he sat down as Joe got to his feet.

'Just now somebody said "Jim's made a nice lad". Ah agree wi' that, but ah can't tek much credit fer it, Alice is the one that's done it. Ralph were reight when 'e said she's a lovely lass, an' if Jim dun't mek 'er a good 'usband, 'e'll 'ave me ter reckon wi'. Anyway, ah'd like ter thank everybody fer their 'elp.'

Henry put in his threepenn'orth in much the same vein, and ended by saying, 'And I won't be losin' a daughter, I'll be gainin' a bedroom'. Finally it was Jim's turn.

He stood and gazed round at the assembled guests. 'There are so many people who've done so much and given us such grand presents that I can't thank them all, but I must give thanks to my parents for puttin' up with me for twenty years, and also to Mr and Mrs Wilson for giving me a wonderful bride. Most of all, I want to thank Mary for makin' a lad from Darnall the happiest man in the world.'

The trestle tables were cleared and the Barnsley Bitter began to flow. Joe was heard to remark to a waiter, 'This ale's as flat as a fart', but as the evening progressed he seemed to get the taste, and manfully soldiered on. At nine o'clock George made his apologies to Jim and Mary. He wanted to get off while the moon was up, ''Cause there's no gaslamps up our way', and offered to give John a lift. John, in his usual courtly manner, said goodbye to his hosts.

As he was leaving, Bolsover told Jim, 'For this week, if tha can gerrin fer t'milkin', ah can manage t'rest.'

Henry, who was close by, chimed in, 'An' Mary, I won't expect to see you at work this week.'

The girl came across and kissed him, protesting, 'But Dad, you can't manage on your own. In any case, you can't do the wages book.'

'All right, I'll bring the book home an' you can do it, but don't expect to get paid'. He smiled as he said it.

Jim prudently restricted his intake of alcohol, and was content to dance with the bride as the pianist churned out waltzes, two-steps and polkas. For them, the evening flew by. The two sets of parents stayed behind to clear up the debris and urged the young couple to be on their way. They said goodnight, and as Jim kissed his mother she whispered, 'Don't rush things with 'er son', and he patted her shoulder reassuringly. The newly-weds strolled home in the starlight, not hurrying. They had a lifetime ahead of them.

★   ★   ★

Jim unlocked the door of number thirty-eight, swept Mary up in his arms and carried her in. He set her down carefully and picked his way in the dark, waving his hand in front of him. He found the chain to the gaslight, struck a match and pulled, and the harsh glare revealed a scene of devastation with bare floorboards and two rolls of lino keeping company with sundry pieces of furniture. He stood and ran his fingers through his hair. 'Good Lord, Mary, look at this lot.' On the positive side, Lily Burrows had lit a fire in the grate, and a kettle was on the hob.

'Ignore it love, we've got plenty of time. How would you like a cup of tea?'

Warming his hands at the fire, Jim replied, 'Yes please, Mary, but I don't want anything to eat.' She poured the tea and handed him a pot.

In a stiff, unnatural voice he said,   'Shall we take it upstairs?' Mary nodded, and he said, 'If you want to go up, I'll just lock the door, and I'll be with you'. Blue eyes met brown and Mary shook her head firmly.

'No, Jim love, we'll go together. I don't want to be parted from you ever again.' She gave a little giggle. 'But you go first this time, I don't trust you.'

Together they climbed the stairs. He lit an oil lamp beside the bed and they gazed at the brass bedstead and rose quilt that Jim had insisted on buying. Wordlessly, they undressed in the warm glow of the oil lamp. Soft shadows caressed her firm, young body, making it a thing of wonder to her untutored lover as slowly they came together in the eternal dance of the sexes. It was early morning before the glow faded in the upstairs window and the name of Whiteley was assured of a future.

Chapter Eleven

* *

THERE FOLLOWED many hours of whitewashing, distempering and papering, and the curtains, made on Jane's sewing machine, were hung ceremonially. Shining linoleum covered the bare boards and a home-made rug lay in front of the gleaming brass fender in the parlour. On the Saturday evening, the young people, their labour of love over, sat in companionable silence on the sofa. The firelight glinted on Mary's precious things arranged on the big, old dresser, and the lustres donated by her grandmother cast rainbows on the heavy flowered wallpaper. Jim stared into the fire, his expression unreadable, and Mary, her bright head on his shoulder, stirred and murmured, 'Penny for 'em, darling'.

He awoke from his reverie and threw his arms around her shoulders. 'I was sittin' here thinkin' that for once in my life I've got everythin' I need, and I just can't believe it's happenin'.'

'Don't get too pleased with yourself, we've got a lot of work to do to keep things as they are. It's back to the grind on Monday.'

Jim grinned. 'Shurrup, I've got to repair all that fencin' round t'farm, an' I'm expectin' Molly droppin' her calf anytime. I might have to stop all night with her when she's due. It'll take me an' George to handle that one.'

Mary sat up and stared at him accusingly. 'We're only just married and you're talking about spending the night with another woman. We'll have to get a divorce.'

Jim chuckled. 'You've nowt' to worry about, we're only good friends.' Once more they settled down, and he continued, 'Y'know . . . George hasn't got any relatives to leave t'farm to . . . an' 'e might leave it to me.'

'Dreams, love, dreams', and she nestled closer. 'I'm quite happy with what I've got.'

★   ★   ★

Between the house, farm and his political activities, Jim found himself stretched to the limit. Mary helped all she could, keeping track of his meetings, committees and so on, while he involved himself with the unions and became a well-known figure at their offices, mostly at the instigation of Taylor. The name 'Big Jim' was becoming known in Labour's corridors of power and it became tacitly understood that he would be a key man in Labour's push for supremacy in the city. His marriage to Mary was an asset to his career, placing the final brick in the solid structure of his public image.

One warm May evening, Jim had a rare break from his campaign, and asked his wife if she would like to go for a stroll in the park, followed by a drink at the *Bradley*. Walking along Staniforth Road, a small stout woman approached and stopped in front of them. It was Mrs Jordan, now a grey-haired sixty-one, but still active in the field of midwifery, as indicated by the black bag she carried.

She said in her no-nonsense voice, 'Evenin', Jim. Is this your new wife? I've been wantin' to meet 'er.' Jim introduced Mary to the woman who had been responsible for his entry into the world.

She looked into Mary's eyes and asked, bluntly, 'How far on is it?'

Mary was nonplussed. 'How far on is what?'

Impatiently, Annie asked, 'Didn't yer mother tell yer about the birds an' bees? 'Ave yer missed this month?'

Mary, blushing and glancing at her husband, answered reluctantly, 'Well, I am a bit late.'

'Aye, ah thought so.' The old woman nodded her head. 'It shows in yer face, ah can allus tell. Ah'll see yer in January.' She stomped off up the road as the couple stood and looked at each other in amazement.

Mary, breathless, asked in an awed voice, 'Is she a witch?'

'No, but is she right?'

'Well, I only had a little show last month, and I am a week late now. I wonder if she is right?' The mental turmoil showed on Jim's face.

'She's t'midwife that delivered me, an' she's not often wrong. You'll have to go an' see Shaughnessy.'

★   ★   ★

Doctor Shaughnessy, his face a map of Ireland, listened, smiling, to Mary's story.

'Roight, me girl', he said, in the brogue that twenty years in Sheffield had hardly touched, 'let's see if th'ould besom's roight', and he smiled. 'It's rarely she's wrong.' He questioned Mary and examined her, then sat back in the old swivel chair, his smile broadening,

'Shure, an' Annie must have the soight. I'll need a sample, but I think you can tell your ould man that he'll be a father in January. If ye have any queer pains, come and see me. Good luck, me girl.'

Mary walked out of the surgery to where Jim was waiting, impatient, and he jumped up as she came out.

'What's he say, love?' The smiling face of his wife told him all. She looked round at the crowd in the waiting room, grabbed his arm and led him outside. Once in the street, Mary confirmed what her eyes had already told him and, stunned, he walked on in silence for long seconds, then burst out,

'I'm scared, Mary. There's so many things that can go wrong, an' I wouldn't forgive myself if anythin' happened to you.'

'Jim, love, don't fret. I'm a strong healthy girl and I'll have a strong healthy baby for you.' Now, stop wittling.

Jim was quiet again for a while, then said, 'I think we'll call him John Joseph. John for Mr Cartwright and Joseph for my dad.'

Mary remonstrated, 'Hold your horses, *I'm* doing the job, and *I* say she's going to be Mary Jane, so there!'

Jim was doubtful. 'I suppose it *could* be a girl, but I wouldn't be able to teach her to play football or take her for a pint when she's old enough.'

Mary was contrite. 'Sorry, love, I never thought. I'll try and have a boy, but don't blame it on me if it isn't.' She paused. 'Has anybody in your family ever had twins?' Jim was aghast.

'Don't even think about it – a penny bun'd cost fourpence.'

That night, under the rose quilt as Jim laid a gentle hand on Mary's nicely-rounded stomach, he murmured, 'It's hard to believe that in there is a little thing that'll likely grow up into a big awkward sod like me.'

'Or a beautiful girl like me', Mary giggled. 'Give it a couple of months and he'll be kicking you, then you'll be sorry.' She rolled over to him. 'Oh Jim, I do love you.'

He lay there, her breath warm on his chest. 'Y'know, Mary, I've just realised, when a man gets a son, it's sort of an immortality, to know that when you're gone, somebody with your name's goin' to be able to do the things you didn't get around to.' Two strong arms enfolded her and two eager bodies fused in warm darkness.

★   ★   ★

A delighted Joe, like Jim, assumed that the child was sure to be a boy, but was soon disabused by Alice and Mary who were both discussing nappies, liberty bodices and all the other esoterica of baby-care. Alice was sorting through knitting patterns as father and son took a celebratory drink from the reserve bottle of whisky.

Later, in the pub, Albert Taylor was delighted, both about the wedding and the coming birth. 'This is the one thing that was missing, Jim. People like to see a family man standing for public office ... but your wife must be right behind you or it's no good.'

'She's behind me, Albert, every inch of the way. If I don't make it, it won't be her fault. She's my secretary, treasurer, and when I need it, she's got some good ideas on publicity. Added to this, she keeps me warm in bed. You must meet her, she's a grand girl.'

Albert laughed. 'I must meet her, it sounds as if she can walk on water. What I really wanted to talk to you about are the rumours that are circulatin' on the Town Hall telegraph. There's nothin' out in the open yet, but some people have been gettin' tenders that shouldn't have, and Percy Brown's name's been whispered as one o' the councillors involved. Now all this is strictly confidential, but if he gets the chop, there'll be a by-election in Darnall, an' I want you in there with a good majority. Don't expect it next week, it could be months before the news becomes public property. But get ready, son, it could be your big chance.'

Albert Taylor supped up and said, 'I'll have to go now, so give my regards to your good lady.'

Week by week, Mary's waistline increased, her only complaint being that nothing fitted her. She bloomed like a flower, glowing with health, and Jim threatened to tie her down if she didn't take it easy. He was wasting his breath, because when she heard about the imminent election, she was full of ideas for making 'Big Jim' the best-known name in Darnall.

'We'll want posters in the pubs and the shops. The fish and chip shops'd be a good place. While they're waiting in the queue, they've got nothing else to look at. Then there's the newspaper boys, they could put leaflets through the letterboxes.' Jim held up his hand.

'Whoa girl, it won't be for a long while yet. And in any case, nothing must leak out until it's in the papers. We can't even get the posters printed until I'm nominated.'

'I know, Jim love, but we've got to be ready when it comes.'

September arrived, and, as Jim brought in the last load of the second hay crop, the rain came down in drops the size of half-crowns. He made his way to the milking shed and was pleasantly surprised to find George finishing the evening milking.

'Thanks, George, that saves me a job.' The farmer grinned up from where he sat, astride the stool, his forehead against Molly's flank and a flat cap on back to front.

'I 'aven't been pullin' my weight Jim, and I felt a bit better, so ah thought ah'd give yer an early night.' He got up, the brimming pail in his hand. ''Ow is Mary, by the way?' Jim grinned and mimed a fat stomach.

'Big, George, big. I think he's goin' to be the first two-stone baby in Darnall.'

'Don't 'ang about then, get off 'ome while yer've chance.'

'Right, so long', and Jim set off home, the rain still siling down like stair-rods. As he passed the 'Iron Duke', the paper-girl was sheltering in the doorway, so he picked up a *Star*, stuck it under his coat and hurried home.

When he came through the back door he was dripping water and Mary, concerned, exclaimed, 'Come on, get those clothes off.'

Jim bridled. 'Oh Mary, can't you wait till we get to bed?'

She giggled. 'You've done enough damage already. Now don't be silly, love, you'll catch your death of cold.'

Jim threw the unread paper on the table and stripped to vest and pants in the scullery, then retired to the bedroom for dry clothes. When he came back into the kitchen he found his wife sitting in the chair reading the paper.

Sternly he asked, 'Hey, woman, what about my tea?'

Mary said nothing, just turning the paper so that he could see the big black headlines. which shouted,

COUNCIL CORRUPTION

Earlier today, our municipal correspondent at the Town Hall heard allegations of irregularities with regard to tenders awarded to contractors. It is believed that large sums of money are involved. As yet, no names have been mentioned, but . . .

The report went on to give vague hints of illegal building transactions said to have taken place. Jim gave a whoop and kissed Mary soundly. 'This is it, love. I'm on my way to the Town Hall. Those Tories don't know what's coming to them!'

★   ★   ★

In successive issues of the local papers, the story was re-hashed, but eventually died a natural death when no more information was available. However, in November, there were once more banner headlines, this time naming the culprits and adding that there would be resignations and by-elections in the wards involved.

At the next Labour Party meeting, Jim went along with Mary who, far from being ashamed of her condition, was proud of the visible signs of the incipient birth. Entering the hall, they were met by Albert Taylor, and Jim did the introductions. The Labour leader shook hands with Mary and said, 'I've been wanting to speak with you, Mrs Whiteley. By the way Jim spoke about you, I expected you at least to have wings. I'd like to congratulate you on the comin' happy event. I hope you know you're married to a future councillor!'

Mary smiled. 'Maybe, but I still have to remind him to change his socks.'

Taylor laughed and turned to Jim. 'Now we can get on with your campaign. We can finance you to a certain extent, but if you wish to contribute, no one's goin' to complain.'

Jim gave a wry grin. 'Could you address yourself to my agent, Albert', pointing to Mary, 'she's got it all organised'.

'Right', said Albert, 'you go and attend to business, and we'll get your campaign sorted out'.

The meeting came to order and Jim helped Charlie Bowers to deal with the routine matters, while Albert and Mary had their heads together. Just before the end of the meeting, he managed to get back to where the two were still talking. Mary had filled four pages of her notebook with information, and as Jim strolled up Taylor said, 'With a personality like yours and Mary backing you, you're as good as in. The moment I know the date of the election, I'll let you know. I've told your wife that Charlie Bowers'll arrange for some helpers, and

103

we've got meetings arranged in the local schools and halls. Anyway, your missus'll tell you all about it, she's got it all down.' He stood up and put on his trilby then slapped Jim on the back. 'So long then, Big Jim, I know you can do it.'

Two weeks later, as he was sitting down to tea, a knock came at the door. It was Charlie Bowers with a letter from Taylor. It read,

Dear Jim,

You can start selling Big Jim on the 22nd. Your opponent is Cyril Burton, a crafty sod. I think the Tories have got wind of you, and they're bringing out their big guns, but don't worry, we're confident that you'll get about seventy percent of the vote. I'll try and get to your campaign meetings, even if it's only to introduce you. Anything else you need, see Charlie. Good Luck.

Albert

While Jim was reading the letter, Mary was mashing and they sat round the kitchen table with a pot of tea as Charlie Bowers talked. 'I've ordered the posters and the leaflets that Mary wanted – it might cost you a few quid o'er what the Party can provide.'

Mary answered, 'That's all right, Charlie, I'll see the bills get paid'.

'There you are', Jim exclaimed, 'she's taken me over! All I need to do is talk. She tells me where I'm goin' and what time – she doesn't gi' me a minute's peace!'

'Yer lucky, all my missus does is play 'ell 'cause I'm out so much. She'll be like a bear wi' a sore 'ead when t'election's on.'

★   ★   ★

Jim's first attempt at wooing the Tory diehards took place at the Darnall Medical Aid Hall at the top of Irving Street. As he mounted the rostrum and looked down at the audience, many of whom he knew, he felt his first misgivings. These were not Labour Party members, they were ordinary people, many of whom had always voted Tory, and he had to bring them round to his way of thinking. As he stood, irresolute, a voice from the audience shouted, 'Leave us a pint then, Jim!'.

It broke the spell. He shouted 'Right, Bill. And 'ow about you, Mrs Williams? The usual?', then held up his hands for order. As they settled down he began.

'Ladies and Gentlemen – or should I call you friends? Tonight I'm not here to sell milk, I'm here to sell the Labour Party, and believe me, you couldn't find a better bargain. Mind you, I think the Tories have done a great job – if you live in Fulwood or Ecclesall. But if you live in Darnall and you're on starvation wages or you're unemployed and livin' on relief, you can't afford to vote Tory. It'd be suicide'

He carried on, to outline his policies on education and housing, then returned to his pet subject. 'You, the working people, are the lifeblood of industry, yet you're treated like cattle by the gaffers. 'Ow many of you have relatives who are ill or even dyin' from bronchitis, asthma or tuberculosis?' Many hands were raised.

'And 'ow many of you have kids with rickets?' Once more, there was a massive show of hands. He spread his arms wide.

'Most of these troubles have been caused by the poisons that pour out of the forest of factory chimneys all around us. The bosses aren't even tryin' to do anythin' about it, an' *you're* payin' with your lives for the big houses in the West End, where the gaffers are breathing clean air.

The average age when a man dies down here in the smoke is fifty, but up Ecclesall they live to the ripe old age of seventy and more.'

He rested his hands on the desk and leaned toward his listeners. 'I've stood up at Hyde Park on a Sunday an' looked down an' seen the whole city spread out.' He slammed the table with his fist. 'On a weekday you can't even see it for the poison cloud that hangs over it, an' twenty-four hours a day we're all breathin' that muck!'

He spat out the word and jabbed with his finger. 'And it's killin' you – an' you – an' you! Believe me, friends, each day a bit of each one of us dies and the bosses are to blame. I've talked to doctors from Rivelin to Rotherham, an' they all agree.'

One member of the audience rose to his feet. 'Ah think yer talkin' a load o' rubbish. Ah've been in t'steel trade all me life, an' ther's nowt wrong wi' me.'

Jim peered at his heckler in the gloom of the hall. 'Oh aye, it's Harry Clark. Let me see, your father died last year, didn't he?' The man nodded. 'And what did he die of?'

Clark, caught off-balance, replied, 'T'doctor said it were bronchitis . . . '

His voice tailed off and Jim stepped in. 'Yes, mate, bronchitis caused by breathin' the fumes from that Siemens furnace at Cammell's.' He stopped and gazed round at his audience as they sat spellbound, then raised an admonitory finger.

'It's our God-given right to breathe clean air an' see the sun, but as long as the gaffers are allowed to do as they like you're goin' to carry on sufferin'.' He once more brought his fist down on the table. 'I pledge my life that I won't rest until Sheffield's clean!'

There were seconds of silence as his graphic prose still gripped them, and he thought he'd failed. Then there was a patter of applause that quickly swelled into a storm.

When it finally died he said. 'While I'm up here, I might as well do somethin' for my livin'. I can't sing or tell jokes, but I can answer questions if you've got any.' After a pause, a small fat man whose bald head shone in the dim light held up his hand and remarked, 'These Tories that you're runnin' down are buildin' a new corporation estate on t'Manor, so they can't be all that bad.'

'You're right, they are. An' have you heard what everybody's callin' the Manor estate? They're callin' it t'consumption estate. It's bein' used like an isolation ward to send people to whose lungs they've ruined.'

The questions came thick and fast, but Jim managed to deal with them all. When the flow finally petered out he continued, 'Now – I've given you a hundred good reasons why you can't afford to vote Tory. So, on polling day I'll expect to see all of you puttin' your cross at the side of 'Big Jim Whiteley', and, thank you for listenin'.'

He came down from the stage floating on the euphoria of success and receiving back-slapping congratulations from people he didn't even know. Near the door were Albert Taylor and Mary, and Jim asked, What're you doin' still here? I thought you'd got somewhere else to go.'

Taylor, his trilby on the back of his head, grabbed Jim's hand in both of his and exclaimed, 'That speech was terrific. I was only stayin' to listen to the start, but once you got goin' I couldn't leave. But I'll have to go now. So long, Jim, and keep up the good work.' He dashed out of the hall.

Mary was ecstatic. 'I've never been so proud, love.' She patted the substantial bulge at the front of her coat. 'Even John Joseph liked it, the way he was kicking.'

'I don't care how much he kicks, he can't come out yet.'

Mary laughed, holding her stomach. 'Don't be too sure, Jim. When he's ready he'll be out, and you'd better be ready to catch him.'

★   ★   ★

Christmas came and went in a whirl of activity, with Jim spending all his spare time canvassing the area. On the evening of January the ninth, the eve of polling day, he made his last attempt to seduce the Tory voters. The meeting was held at the Labour Hall, and if attendances were anything to go by, he reckoned his chances were good, as there were only a few seats left when he entered the hall.

He felt strangely deserted, as it was the first time that Mary had not attended. The strangeness persisted until he looked down from the rostrum and, in the middle of the front row, saw Ralph. His pipe was clamped between crooked teeth and he grinned as he gave Jim a thumbs-up. It gave him the lift he needed, and he tackled the tough audience with gusto. The result was a repeat of his first meeting and he came away with Ralph, buoyed up by his seeming triumph.

After a quick two pints at the club, he went home, where Mary demanded a blow-by-blow account of the evening's activities, after which she allowed herself to be put to bed with a hot brick wrapped in flannel. Jim soon joined her, but his thoughts of the next day wouldn't allow him to sleep at first. Eventually, though, he drifted off, with a melange of hopes and fears haunting his dreams.

At six on the morning of polling day, Jim was sitting on the stool in the milking shed, feeling the rough texture of Molly's teats as he alternately pulled and squeezed. As the rich, creamy liquid jetted into the bucket, his thoughts went involuntarily to the coming ballot. The old stone-built school would open soon, and close at nine o'clock that night, and he would be there to watch the count. Barring accidents, he should know by 10.30 if he was a councillor. He put it to the back of his mind, and for the rest of the morning threw himself into his farmwork.

During the afternoon and early evening, Jim went out on the knocker, reminding folk in areas where he thought they should vote for him that they should make the effort and go out to the polling station and do just that. From their house, Mary organised teams of canvassers to do the same thing in other parts of the ward, so that as much of the likely Labour vote that could be got out was encouraged to do so. It wasn't always easy, for even Labour supporters who'd got home from a long day shift at three o'clock or later wanted no more than to get their heads down for an hour or two.

Eventually, Jim returned home at eight o'clock. He'd done the evening's milking and with people putting their children to bed it was no time to be still knocking on their doors. He forced himself to eat his tea on Mary's urgings. She also mentioned that she'd been having some queer twinges.

Jim was uneasy. 'If you have any trouble while I'm out, pop round and get Alice to go for Mrs Jordan. I'll be home as soon as I can.'

'All right, old worry-guts, I'll behave. But don't stay away too long, love, I need you near me.'

At five minutes to nine, Jim, dressed in his best, with rosette in buttonhole, was off to his date with destiny. As he walked up Whitby Road he saw his Conservative opponent, Cyril Burton, coming along the opposite kerb. It was the first time he'd seen him in the flesh and, as Burton crossed the road, he sensed the aura of confidence that oozed from the man. They eyed each other like strange dogs, stiff-legged and hair bristling.

Mr Burton's suit was bespoke quality, and in fact the whole ensemble, from velour trilby to snowy spats, shouted prosperity. Across his ample stomach hung a heavy gold watch chain, and broken veins in his cheek and nose betrayed a fondness for the bottle. He held out a plump hand , heavy with rings, and said, 'So you're Big Jim. I've been wanting to meet you. I'm Cyril Burton, "man of the people", as it says on the posters!'

Jim took the proffered hand. The sweaty handshake was as false as a three-pound note, as was the whole manner of this professional politician.

Jim felt an instinctive revulsion, and as the other hand gripped his, harder

107

than was necessary, the muscles of his forearm knotted and he squeezed until the bones creaked. The painted smile stayed nailed on Burton's face, but behind the eyes Jim glimpsed the red hatred of the animal as some of the colour left the florid cheeks.

They strolled on up the flagged pavement, the stones cockled and tilted. Cyril looked up the six inches to meet Jim's eyes and, massaging his injured paw, said, 'Big Jim, eh? Well, the bigger they come, the harder they fall.'

'Yes', replied Jim, 'but first you've got to hit 'em'. They entered the hall together and saw the long trestle tables where people were busily emptying the black ballot boxes prior to counting. The candidates were furnished with cups of tea and installed in two uncomfortable school chairs at one end of the hall. Around them lay the mats, forms and other gym tackle and they waited in ill-concealed impatience as the piles of votes mounted.

At half-past-ten, the self-important figure of the returning officer threaded his way along the aisles, pausing at each station and painstakingly writing in his book. He returned to the platform and sat down once more at the table there, poring over his figures. As he laboured, the flustered figure of Albert Taylor burst into the hall, coat open and flying. 'Sorry, Jim, dead horse on the tram-linest in t'Wicker, we were stuck there for half-an-hour.'

Cyril Burton smirked. 'I think you've had a wasted journey, Albert.'

Taylor glared across at the grinning Tory. 'I've heard ducks fart before, Cyril, so you're whistlin' in the wind.'

The returning officer's voice cut through the hubbub. 'If you two gentlemen'd kindly get on the stage, ah'll announce the results of the poll.' They mounted the rostrum and stood, one each side of the official as he dramatically called out the results.

'I will now announce the results of the Darnall by-election for January tenth, 1923. Cyril Burton, 1,652 votes. James Henry Whiteley, 1,718 votes. Therefore, I hereby declare that James Henry Whiteley duly elected councillor for Darnall ward.'

There was clapping from the body of the hall and a wild war-whoop from Taylor as he dashed over and slapped an elated Jim on the back. 'You're in, Jim, we licked the bastards – sorry, Cyril, present company excepted.'

With a grudging, 'The best man won, Jim, all the best', Burton left the hall, defeated. As soon as he decently could, Jim dashed out of the hall and ran all the way home. Bursting through the back door he saw Mary pacing the kitchen, both hands in the small of her back. She looked at him with pain-filled eyes and pleaded, 'Rub my back, Jim love, it's giving me hell – that's it, press on, hard. Oh, that's better, keep it up.'

Alice came in as he was ministering to his wife and said, 'Ah've just been for some milk, son, we've mashed four times since you went. Annie's been an' she's comin' back at twelve o'clock. T'pains are every twelve minutes, so it shouldn't be long. Oh, sorry love, 'ow did yer go on?'

Jim, without turning round, answered, 'I won, Mam', and carried on rubbing, his face concerned. Mary, in spite of the pain, turned to him and exclaimed, 'You *won!*' and kissed him. 'That's wonderful Jim. Ow, rub again, love.' Alice was over the moon.

'Councillor Whiteley', she savoured the sound of it, 'Ah must get a paper in t'mornin'. You'll be in it, won't yer?'

★   ★   ★

The cold light of the full moon was silvering the old terraced houses on Kirby Road, and the little plump woman, a shawl tight round her head and shoulders against the chill, trudged along a pavement which was clean and white with fresh-fallen snow. She reached number thirty-eight and a wedge of light slanted across the pavement as she was admitted

Then the street was once more deserted except for the row of footprints, black on white, left by the old-fashioned high button boots.

Half-an-hour later, from the bright orange rectangle of the bedroom window came a despairing cry as the newest member of the Whiteley family was forced out into the cruel world. John Joseph had joined the human race.

At the same moment, three miles away in the cabin in the woods, the same moon, peering through the window, starkly illuminated the prone figure of John Cartwright. The already gaunt body seemed to deflate, as what men call the soul left its temporary accommodation and the light went out of those compelling eyes forever. The cycle was complete.

Epilogue: 1980

* *

T HE BRIGHT SUN of late morning bathed the city below, as Jim Whiteley
sat on the bench on Hyde Park, leaning on his stick and contemplating
the shining towers of modern Sheffield. He had caught the bus up from
his home at Oaks Farm, where his son, John Joseph, and the family were running the business.

Truth to tell, Jim didn't have a lot to do with the work, for at the ripe old age
of seventy-seven he was quite willing to leave things to his three sons and their
grandsons. When the diabetes that had been eating George Bolsover finally
claimed him, Jim had been left with the farm. His mind, still lucid, travelled
back down the long years of strife and satisfaction, through the climaxes and
depressions, the successes and disasters. He decided that, on the whole, it had
been worthwhile.

Viewing the panorama through the clear air he spoke softly to himself. 'It
took us long enough, Mary, but we did it, the city can breathe.' Any reply must
have been heard by him alone, for the seat beside him was empty.

He recalled the ones that he'd left along the way: John Cartwright, put to
rest as snow lay on the coffin top; Alice, gone to meet her beloved Joe at the age
of seventy, unable to go on alone. And finally Mary, who had died in Western
Park Hospital only three years earlier. Jim had never really recovered from his
loss.

His thoughts melted imperceptibly into dreams, and the old eyes closed as
the shadows lengthened across the homes of distant Pitsmoor.

★   ★   ★

The shadows were long when the young couple came walking arm-in-arm
along the path from Skye Edge. As they neared the seat, the girl said sympa-
thetically, 'Look at that old man. He's fallen asleep. He'll be cold when he
wakes up.'

Her young man tapped the thin shoulder and said, 'You'll be gettin' cold,
Dad'. Jim toppled gently sideways, lying as if asleep. Wherever Mary had gone,
Jim was now with her, his long day over.